I0586884

ESSENTIAL MAGIC

THE FAY OF SKYE - BOOK ONE

CARA MCKINNON

Stars and Stone Books

Cover Design by Stars and Stone Books
Editing by Literally Yours Editing

Stars and Stone Books

Digital Edition 1.2
Print Edition 2

Digital ISBN: 978-09977081-0-3
Print ISBN: 978-0-9989514-2-3

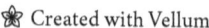 Created with Vellum

For Steve.

It's dangerous to go alone, so I walk beside you.

29 April 1874

My wee one hasn't moved in hours. I can feel her there inside me, her little life force so strong and hot, but like any new mother I worry. I've seen many a stillborn babe who was energetically kicking its mother the night before. I miss Gran. She would have known what to do. She told me, if anything happened, to send word to her kin in England. I found an old letter from her sister, Beatrice —sent after the War Between the States, making sure she was all right—and so I wrote to her today. I don't know what I expect in answer. I don't even know that I wish for them to be aware of me, or my child. Gran left England because they cared more about position than love, and I don't want a child of mine stifled by that world. Still—I am the last Fay in America. I worry for her future here, too.

-from the journal of Aileana Fay Cook

Etta Mae Cook stepped from the passenger car onto the platform in Waterloo Station and stumbled.

After Raleigh, she thought she'd be prepared for London. She'd expected urbanity—the magical energy raised by hundreds of thousands of people living in close proximity. She hadn't understood.

Any piece of earth long inhabited by humans will absorb something of the nature and the character of its people. And this bit—this city on the river—had been walked by mankind for thousands of years.

The weight of years past and lives lived left her gasping and disoriented.

Bodies jostled her from all sides, but she inhaled and sought her center, reaching down into herself to that point of balance and harmony that tied her soul to her flesh. The power there hummed and danced. She exhaled and pulled the energy outward until it suffused her limbs and her skin.

Etta dragged another breath into her lungs, redolent with coal smoke and her fellow travelers. The reminder of here and now anchored her. She released the breath.

Calm. Peace. Unity. Determination.

The day her mother died six weeks ago, her life had shifted from its predictable course in Appalachia and gone careening and wheeling to places she could not yet imagine. London was not the first step, and it would not be the last, but it was the biggest yet.

Maintaining her balance, keeping a hold on her valise, and not making a major social gaffe were the most important things now. Or maybe they were all the same thing.

Please, by all that is sacred and true, let them not think me a fool.

A sharp voice shattered her introspection, the consonants clipped and staccato. "Are you Miss Cook?"

Etta squashed the urge to flinch, and though she would have liked to bolt back to the train, she forced her feet to move toward the speaker.

She'd expected to be met by a servant, but no maid wore silk and velvet, or carried herself with such a haughty mien. This must be Lady Cecily Seward, the Marchioness of Hazelby.

The woman was younger than she'd thought, not much older than Etta's mother had been. Her dark hair was swept up in a simple arrangement, with only a few sprinklings of grey through the brown strands save for a streak of silver at the upper left temple that disappeared beneath a small-brimmed hat.

That pale streak marked this sharp-tongued English-woman as family. Ma used to call it the "Mark of Fay."

"I am Etta Mae Cook," she said, enunciating precisely, careful of her accent.

For a tense, uncertain moment, they stared at each other. There were other similarities to Ma. Hazel eyes—though the marchioness had a mix of brown, blue, and grey where Ma's had been green, gold, and brown. A strongly bowed upper lip that Etta had not inherited, matched with a full lower one that Etta shared. Dark arching brows and strong cheekbones, though not as high as Etta's.

This woman's magic had a different feel, though—like a solitary boulder rising up from a field, its edges smoothed by wind and rain, but still resolute. Ma's had been a blackberry bramble—all canes and thorns—studded with brilliant white flowers and sweet fruit. But though their power was not in any way the same, this woman was as strong as Ma had been.

"Come with me." The woman pivoted and walked off into the crowd of disembarked passengers. She said nothing else, made no gesture of welcome, and did not watch to see that Etta complied with her order.

Etta grabbed her valise and strode after her. Her skirts hampered her steps as she strove to keep sight of the woman in the mass of shifting people. After only moments of brisk walking, the constriction of her new corset left her gasping and breathless. But she endured, and soon they were out of the station and onto a busy street.

Cabs and omnibuses drawn by horses stopped and started near the walkway, picking up and dislodging passengers. Here and there a private carriage stood in the jostling line, awaiting wealthier clients.

The smells were unfamiliar and almost as bad as the weight of two thousand years of magic. Every breath held an underlay of brine, sewage, and fish, covered by the stronger odors of horse manure, coal smoke, and the general stink of humanity. Etta forced down a gag.

The woman halted near the edge of the walk. Etta stopped a few steps behind, unsure whether it would be poor manners to approach her and attempt to speak. While she hesitated, a voice hailed her from behind.

This new figure was small and fine-boned, a tiny doll of a woman with a matching round face, large eyes, and rosebud mouth. She and Etta had shared both the boat from America and the train from the port, but she'd said farewell inside the car and Etta hadn't thought to see her again.

"Hello, Mrs. Upton."

"Are you in need of a conveyance, Miss Cook? I'm happy to share my carriage and take you wherever you need to go."

"Oh, no. I—"

"Good afternoon, Lady Falcestershire."

Etta glanced over at the other woman—the marchioness? —who obviously knew Mrs. Upton.

Or, Etta thought with annoyance, *not Mrs. anything. Lady.*

"Lady Hazelby! What a surprise. What brings you to the train station?"

So she *was* the Marchioness of Hazelby. Etta ought to feel comforted by the confirmation, but the two women eyed each other with animosity. *Back away quietly. They look like bull deer about to rut.*

The marchioness glanced at Etta, then back to Lady F— What was it again?

"I have come to collect Miss Cook. She will be…staying with me, for a short time."

"How delightful!" Lady F's tone was so bright it made the audible equivalent of staring into the sun. It was also patently false. Underneath the forced brilliance, Etta suspected she was brimming over with curiosity. She wanted to know their connection, and how a poor American witch had managed to secure an invitation to stay in the household of the Marquess of Hazelby.

"Quite," Lady Hazelby replied. She glanced to the drive, and then back to Lady F. "Ah, my carriage has arrived. It won't do to keep the horses standing. Good day, Lady Falcestershire."

"Good day Lady Hazelby. Miss Cook."

They all inclined their heads in a round-robin of polite gestures, and Lady Hazelby led Etta toward the carriage. A man climbed from his perch on the outside of the vehicle to help the marchioness inside, and then held his arm out to Etta. She didn't think she needed the help, but it was best to emulate Lady Hazelby. He took her valise and handed her up to the carriage step.

Inside the carriage, Etta settled across from Lady Hazelby. She had to take the seat facing backward, a position which always gave her the oddest sense that she was moving through different levels of the spirit world rather than physical space. At least the cushions were soft. Her train seat had been hard as a rock.

The marchioness stared off into a corner of the carriage,

carefully not looking at Etta.

Outside, Lady Falcestershire still stood, watching them. What was going on here? On the boat, she'd introduced herself as Mrs. Upton. Her accent was English, and she'd boarded in Baltimore, the closest port to Etta with regular steamship service to England. During their entire voyage, the woman had presented herself as a well-to-do commoner, the widow of a wealthy older gentleman who now had the means and freedom to travel. She'd said she'd been visiting family and friends in all of the major east coast cities, from Boston to Washington.

How much of that had been truth? Etta wanted to ask Lady Hazelby, but was terrified to make a social faux pas. The woman already refused to look at her.

Had she done something offensive? Other than the wobble getting down from the train, she'd acted with perfect propriety. Hadn't she? Maybe it was her accent. She'd practiced the way Aunt Rachel spoke, with its soft, swallowed consonants and fluid vowels, but Etta was a mountain girl. Had she unintentionally used her native twang?

Maybe it was her dark skin. Even in the dim interior of the carriage, the other woman's skin had an almost ivory gleam. Etta's natural tone was a warm red-brown, and her dislike of hats meant the sun turned her face even darker. In the mountains, her resemblance to her Choctaw and Cherokee relatives meant the tribes accepted her as a friend, if not a member. Would English society reject her for the same similarity?

How to proceed? At home, she'd have said what she wanted, asked whatever came into her head, and been done. Here, there were rules and strictures, and consequences for breaking those rules. If she did something bad enough, the marchioness might not agree to teach her.

That was not acceptable. Coming to England to learn

magic was Ma's dying wish. She had to convince the Fay clan that she was worthy of training.

The carriage came to a halt before Etta could decide what to say. The door opened, and Lady Hazelby rose to allow the footman to hand her down. Etta followed without waiting for his assistance.

As she walked off the carriage step, the high heel of her unfamiliar, fashionable walking shoe caught in the hem of her just as fashionable and even more unfamiliar walking dress. She stumbled, but managed to steady herself.

What she wouldn't give to be on her mountain right now, striding about in boots and trousers, the way any sensible gods would have intended.

Fashion would not defeat her.

While she awkwardly hopped and lurched to free the heel, the footman hurried to her and caught her arm. With his assistance, she succeeded in planting both absurd shoes onto the walkway.

"Steady, miss," he murmured, low enough that the marchioness—who had marched past a filigreed gate and down a walk toward an impressive townhouse—could not hear.

"Thank you," she whispered back. His kindness gave her strength. Steps deliberate and quick, she strode toward her future.

2

1 November 1875

A letter arrived today from the duchess herself. I hadn't expected that. My great-aunt must have sent her my missive. She begged me to come to her, and to bring my babe. But I cannot. Fayt will never leave these mountains, and I won't go without him. I don't want my daughter raised without a father, and I don't want to live without my husband.

I haven't answered her. I know that I must, and yet—what if Etta needs her, some day? I do not wish to take away any path that would be of use to my lass. I don't know what to do.

Gran, I miss you so much.

-from the journal of Aileana Fay Cook

Cuthbert Malcolm Elliott Seward, second son of the Marquess of Hazelby, known—thank the gods—to his family and friends as Mal, stared into his mother's immaculate garden from the rear terrace and wished he were anywhere but this sooty, cold, monstrosity of a city.

Father had summoned him after he'd instigated another shouting match with the foreman at the family mine in Wales. Mal couldn't regret it, despite the result. The foreman was a soulless nightmare. What had Giles been thinking, to hire a brute that didn't care about the workers or the land?

No, Mal could not have kept his mouth shut once he knew the truth of the conditions inside and outside the mine. But being here was almost worse.

He hated London. Had abhorred every trip here as a boy, into this world of squalor and coal. He'd allowed Bertie and the Marlborough House set to seduce him into their glittering society for a little while, but it hadn't taken long to see the truth. The *ton* was a garish balloon around a lot of hot air.

And sometimes, the balloon was full of flammable gas, and someone lit a match.

Mal shuddered. He wasn't going to think about that right now. Better to think of Scotland, and his land and tenants. They, and the disused mine he'd imagined reopening, were the reason he'd traveled to Wales in the first place.

He'd have gone straight back to Scotland, and damned his father, except that the telegram had threatened to cut off his allowance. With every penny he owned sunk into improvements for his crofters and a mortgage on the property, he couldn't afford to lose access to the family purse.

So he'd come back, and had another three-way argument with Father and Giles in his father's study.

He'd flung an accusing finger first at Father, and then

Giles. "You two can't hear the earth screaming, but I can. If you'd let me hire a geomancer—"

"Those charlatans cost half again as much as my foreman and work crew," Giles interrupted, "and they take twice as long to produce the same yield. It isn't profitable." If he'd been the sort of person who talked with his hands, they'd have been flailing about. As it was, Giles was always collected and contained. He stood with muscles held rigid, his voice strained and his lips pinched.

"Profit." Malcolm flung the word like a curse. He liked movement, so he paced over to Giles, pointing a finger at his elder brother in accusation. "That's all you care about, isn't it?"

"Of course it is."

Both brothers swiveled toward their father. The marquess leaned back in the leather chair behind his desk, giving the appearance of calm and relaxation, but with the barest hint of tension along his jaw. Mal's father usually let them shout each other down before intervening, so he must have grown tired of hearing this particular argument repeated for the thousandth time.

"Our lives depend on money. This house, all of our property, your ramblings, Percy's tuition, and Olivia's travel expenses—all require funds. And there's no profit to be had in land anymore." He steepled his fingers where they rested on his abdomen. He had the tiniest beginnings of a pouch there, but that was to be expected of a man in the latter half of his fifth decade. Otherwise, the elder Seward was fit and hale.

"There isn't a single estate in the kingdom that hasn't been forced to sell off a bit here or there, or the whole thing but the home farm. The few that have managed to hang on are the ones who invested in industry. Now the indolent wrecks who refused to dirty their hands with a trade are seeking money for old rope." The marquess sat up and put his hands on the edge of the big mahogany desk, leaning toward Mal. "How many of your friends from college and university are engaged to American heiresses? Ten?"

"Twelve." Malcolm's mouth turned in a sour expression. The newspapers from New York were calling it *Annus Mirabilis*—a miraculous year—because so many titled or upper-class families had chosen wealthy American girls to bolster their empty coffers. The Latin, Mal thought, was a bit of an exaggeration.

"So." His father smiled at him, but it was the sort of smile that Mal distrusted immediately—too broad and with too much glee. The old man was up to something. "You've got ideas about how to run a mine. Wonderful. If you can pay for them, Giles will implement them."

Giles spluttered, all that tension finally escaping in an undignified expulsion of air. "Wh-what? Father, you can't be serious!"

"He doesn't expect me to come up with the money." Mal stared into his father's blue eyes, mirrors of his own. All three of the men in the room, father and sons, bore a close resemblance. Dark hair, straight noses, wide mouths, and piercing blue eyes. Only Mal looked markedly different, because of the streak of white in his hair. "You're safe, unless I follow in my school chums' footsteps."

Roland Seward, Marquess of Hazelby, grinned. It was a true smile this time, and his eyes crinkled at the corners. He'd always been pleased when Mal could read his intentions, although the gods only knew why. Did he think his son was using magic on him? In the first place, it didn't work that way. And in the second...Mal didn't cast spells anymore. Ever.

"I'd like to see you wed, and settled. If you can find a lady with some money, even better."

At his sides, Mal's fingers closed into fists. He slammed one of those fists onto the desk. "So that's the real reason you called me back to London. Do you have a list of names I should peruse before setting off to view what's for sale on the Marriage Mart? Or no, I forgot. *I'm* the one that's for sale."

Father didn't even have the decency to flinch. Mal's anger only amused him. "Your mother would know better than I."

"I've no interest in silly debutantes, rich or not."

His father shrugged and leaned back again, nonchalance restored. "I honestly don't care if you wed a princess or the poorest crofter's daughter. It seems that Giles and Caroline will have only girls, and I want the succession assured. That means you—and Percy, if necessary—wed and having legal offspring."

Mal didn't look at his brother, but his magical senses caught the tension radiating from him in waves of heat. Giles loved his daughters, but he'd been born with a preponderance of familial duty, and he saw his inability to sire a son to carry on the title as a failure.

Father didn't look at Giles, either. "I'll keep up your quarterly allowance as long as you're actively seeking a bride, and I will double whatever dowry her family offers. If you do choose a poor chit, I'll settle a flat hundred thousand pounds on you both, with another hundred thousand in trust for your heirs."

Mal couldn't keep his jaw from slackening. He'd recently read of an heiress whose family had paid a million pounds for her dowry. He doubted his father could match that, but even the minimum was no small amount of money.

"I suppose you see this as an investment, and children as the profit?"

His father's eyebrows rose, as though to ask, 'are you truly shocked?'

"And if I walk away now? Go to Scotland and hunker down on my bit of land there?"

"Then the money stops. I know you've not got anything liquid at the moment and a mortgage to pay, so don't pretend that's a viable alternative."

He was right, damn his eyes. Why couldn't Giles and Caroline have managed to pop out a son by now? Damn English primogeniture laws anyway. At least in Scotland a daughter would inherit, whether she had uncles or a distant male cousin or not.

"So I'm stuck here until I wed, then?"

The marquess settled his hands on his thighs, his posture still relaxed and open. "Until the end of the season," he corrected. "Then I expect you to accept invitations to as many house parties as are offered. If you're unwed by next season, we'll revisit the arrangement."

"You'll need to fund a new kit." Mal gestured at his suit. It was far from worthy of a ballroom, as he'd not bothered to dress formally in Scotland. Also, he'd filled out quite a bit in muscle after two years of manual labor. None of his old evening wear would fit across the shoulder anymore.

"Of course. And there's one more thing." The casual smile turned down. "Viola's babies." Father didn't like to be reminded of his daughter, who'd nearly had her children out of wedlock because she refused to wed their father. But she and Ian had reconciled—or made their peace, anyway—and agreed to the marriage only a few months ago. She'd been hugely, visibly pregnant during the ceremony, and both sets of parents had worn stoic masks over cheeks gone crimson with humiliation.

She ought to have been left alone. If she didn't want to marry Ian, she shouldn't have been forced into it. Mal had told her as much outside the church, but she'd smiled and told him it was all sorted. Then she'd asked him to cast the binding-spell on them that was the Fay clan version of a wedding ceremony.

He'd refused. He'd already bound them too close.

No, he would *not* think of that.

"What of the twins?" He'd avoided Viola—and Ian—since the wedding. But every child born to Clan Fay was welcomed by the magical members of the family with a special spell, and he had a feeling he knew what was coming next.

New tension lined the marquess's jaw, and his tone was stiff and flat. "Your mother requires that you attend her in Scotland. But you will return once the babies arrive and the…ritual is complete. Is that understood?"

Another thing his father disliked was speaking of magic. He accepted that his wife and two of his children had gifts, but he preferred that those gifts not touch his daily life in any way. Until recently, Mal had not understood how his mother survived.

But he'd managed to go two years without casting a spell, so perhaps his mother wasn't as bothered by the cage of her marriage and society as he'd always assumed.

"There are reasons why…"

"Your mother insists. You will go to Scotland, then come back here and find a wife, or you are cut off."

Mal had bristled, but he truly had no choice. His tenants depended on him to keep the estate afloat until the improvements were finished and they could sustain themselves again. "Fine," he'd said, casting a heated look at first Giles, then his father. "I will agree. For now."

He'd turned and stomped out of the study, flinging the door closed behind him. A few steps took him through the back ballroom and then out onto the terrace, where he now stood, staring into the muted grey light of an overcast London afternoon.

Mal stepped off the slate of the terrace and onto the grass, and nearly fell to his knees.

Something moved up from the earth, shot through his legs, and then slammed into his belly—a force like lightning and a crashing wave at once, shattering inside him and dragging at his soul like sand pulled by the surf. He gasped and trembled, braced for pain but swamped instead with pleasure so intense it threatened to unman him.

He gained control slowly, forcing the sensation back with a steadily increasing effort of will. When he'd mastered himself, he opened his second Sight.

He needed to be wary. He'd had a good reason for giving up active spellwork two years ago. Connecting his magic with anything else after all this time could be catastrophic.

The lines of magic around the house were stable and staid, the energy following the same paths it had traveled in this portion of Town for years. The City of London was laid out following existing magical topography, but from St. James to Regent's Park, the city engineers had tried to restructure the leylines rather than working with them. Mal ground his teeth together. He hated opening his Sight here, hated having to stretch out his senses along the precisely aligned grid rather than the more natural course of the countryside.

There was only one anomaly in the rigid flow of power: a kind of whirl or eddy. He couldn't tell the cause, but it might be centered on a person. Whatever it was—or whoever—was on the other side of the house, near the entryway. He considered running in the opposite direction, but he wasn't a coward. He would deal with this threat to his peace and move on. He strode back inside and through the music room, then down the long hallway toward the foyer.

Strand, the butler, opened the door as Mal rounded the corner, and Mal's first boot-fall struck the marble floor in sync with his mother's entrance. The synchronicity resonated inside of him, and he almost closed his Sight. Sometimes keeping it open made things seem more symbolic and important. Mages had gone mad, using the Sight too often or too long. But he needed to find out what was, even now, pulling at the edges of his magic.

Mother looked startled to see him. She'd been out when he arrived, but he would have expected Father to tell her he was coming.

"Malcolm." She extended a hand to him, and he took it, surprised that she hadn't embraced him. She wasn't the most ebullient or demonstrative of persons, but she usually put her arms around him and kissed his cheek after a long absence. Her stern expression, and the surface emotions that roiled across her aura, revealed consternation rather than welcome. "You're home."

"Hello, Mother," Mal said, and squeezed her fingers.

"Your father was supposed to have you meet me in Scotland. Now is not a good time for you to be here." Her words were low, but distinct.

"He said I'm to go with you to Scotland, but he wants me doing the rounds of the Marriage Mart before and after. I'm to find a chit to wed, or else."

His mother stiffened. Then, over her shoulder, he saw the reason for her reticence. And the reason for the surge of heat, magic, and passion that had nearly crumpled him to the grass.

The woman was not what would be termed an exquisite, or what his grandfather's generation would have styled 'a diamond of the first water.' There was something too primal in her features and her bearing, and her aura shimmered with power. She was a sunset on a mountain peak, or the eerie colors in the sky in the far north of Scotland. She was a vein of gold still glittering inside the rock, her treasure clear but held close, in her own keeping.

She would never belong to anyone but herself, and that made him long for her to share that self with him—in every conceivable way.

He almost laughed, even as he feared what such a connection would mean. *Well, Father, it seems I may have no choice but to follow your orders after all.*

His mother noticed the indiscreet admiration, and the way the woman returned his stare. She frowned, and he knew why. Mal was supposed to avoid magical entanglements. But this woman might prove too much temptation for him to resist.

Mal stepped toward the woman and was halted by a hand on his arm. Why was Mother being so formal? He chafed at the delay and waited for the introduction.

Mother's tone was brittle, the words sharp, clipped, and forced. "Miss Cook, allow me to introduce my son, Lord Cuthbert Seward." Mal frowned at the use of his hated first name, but returned his features to a genial smile when he bowed to Miss Cook. It was a polite bow, of slightly more deference than he might otherwise have used toward a woman of uncertain lineage.

If possible, his mother stiffened further at this evidence of his interest.

"And this is Miss Etta Mae Cook." She said the name as though the sounds of it were acid, burning her tongue.

Miss Cook curtsied. There was nothing precisely wrong with the curtsey, except that she didn't look easy doing it. Something about the way she held herself said she wasn't a woman meant to bow. Her motion caused ripples in the magical currents of the room, and the aroma of rich, fertile earth—like a field plowed and ready for planting—surged in his nostrils. The flavors of honeysuckle and salt cascaded over his tongue.

"I'm pleased to meet you, Miss Cook." From up close, he could see that her eyes were dark brown, with little flecks of green and gold glittering in the depths. Her magic—so full of potential, so warm and alive—pulled at him, strong and inexorable. Was this what Ian felt like when Viola was near?

He closed his Sight, suddenly desperate not to see her brilliance, not to taste and smell and feel her.

"And I you, Lord Cuthbert."

Malcolm winced. "My mother introduced me that way because it's my first name, but everyone uses my middle name, Malcolm."

"Oh," she said, and the sound came out flatter, and higher pitched, than her previous vowels. Almost as if another woman had spoken entirely. In the same faster accent, she said, "I didn't mean to offend, Lord Malcolm." This was her true voice, and it wrapped around his ears and his brain. A purely physical reaction, but one that woke his magic as though he were a teenage boy again, feeling the first swells of puberty and power.

"You didn't," he assured her. He wasn't offended, but his magic was slipping out of his control. He'd never felt such a sudden and overwhelming urge to merge his magic with another's. But he couldn't. Would never do that again. He clamped down on his magical senses even harder than usual, dampening the sensations that were as natural to him as the pressure of air on another person's skin.

He took refuge in humor. "And there's no need to Lord me. I don't care for the courtesy title or the first name. It's my father's fault. He read too much Browning." He smiled at her, and won a small tilt at the corner of her lips in response. Those lips were far too enticing, and made him want to draw her close and discover how well they fit against his. He could fight the magical pull, but what about desire?

She looked away from him, at his mother, and the smile faded.

Mother stood with a frozen expression of polite interest on her face. But beneath the bland exterior, he she seemed ashamed. Or perhaps afraid. He wished Viola was here. With his senses dampened, he couldn't read Mother's aura, and he'd never been the best at interpreting those anyway.

Mal returned his attention to Miss Cook. It wasn't exactly good manners, but he was curious, so he asked, "What brings you to our home, Miss Cook?"

She continued to stare at his mother, so he asked, "Mother, am I missing something?"

"Miss Cook will be our guest for a short time," she answered. "She is a...distant relative, through my great-grandmother Lilias."

Malcolm started. Lilias Fay, first Duchess of Fay, was the most prominent member of his mother's clan—a great seeress and witch who had been instrumental in the war against Napoleon. Her exploits were legend, from leading the group of mages that cast the Great Barrier over the channel, to serving on the Peninsula, to taking the field at Waterloo beside Wellington. She'd then opened schools for magic all across the kingdom, though sadly, most of them were now closed. She'd died at the age of one hundred when Malcolm was thirteen, and he'd mourned her loss ever since.

"How are you related to Lilias?"

The revelation of her relationship to the family had opened a door, allowing Miss Cook to speak. "My great-grandmother was Lilias' youngest daughter, Marianne."

"So you're my..." he paused, counting the generations.

"Some kind of distant cousin." Her expression was pleasant enough, and her tone indicated an attempt at levity, but the humor was tempered by wariness. "We're barely related at all. And I wouldn't impose on your family except..." Her voice trailed off. There was so much pain behind her eyes, but she steadied herself. "Except, my mother died. It was her last wish that I find the rest of the Fay clan to finish my training. I can't study in America because I'm from the South."

He'd heard that magic was outlawed in the southern United States after their civil war, and he'd even met a few Americans who'd come to England to train, but no one had ever approached the family directly. Clan Fay's sort of magic was distinctly out of fashion.

Mal eyed his mother, who still looked like she had stepped in something rank and was trying to pretend the scent was rosewater. "Are you going to train her?"

"I will test her, but I will not make any determinations until after Viola's babes are born."

The twins would be born within a fortnight. Since his father had insisted that he go with the rest of the magically-gifted members of the family to the birthing, he and Mother would leave in a day or so to travel to the Highlands.

Magically-gifted family members, Mal realized, now included Etta Mae Cook.

Mal grinned at his mother. If he had to be miserable on this trip, so could she. "Why doesn't Miss Cook come with us to Scotland?"

≈

TWENTY MILES TO THE WEST AT WINDSOR CASTLE, LADY Amelia Upton, Queen's Sorceress and Dowager Countess of Falcestershire, curtseyed to her queen and took her normal seat, at the left hand of the monarch.

"What have you learned?"

Queen Victoria rarely eschewed a chance to engage in the social niceties. That she had done so now was a window into her discomfort over the American chit.

"She is powerful," Amelia said, "but untrained. Those damn Americans and their laws of attrition."

The queen did not take up the offered tangent. "That could bode well for us. Will she come to you?"

"Not if I don't force the issue. She mentioned to me twice on the voyage that her mother had wanted her to seek out her family. Unless the Fay clan turns her away, she'll stand by them."

"Then you must ensure that they turn her away, and to you."

Amelia inclined her head. She would do whatever must be done to fulfill Her Majesty's desires.

3

26 June 1882

I received a letter today from Great-Aunt Beatrice. The duchess has died. I watch Etta doing her lessons between her chores—see the little callouses on her fingers and the bruising under her eyes from weariness—and I wonder if I made the right choice. She could be living like a queen in England, with servants to wait on her and her every desire granted. It would be a cage, but so is the work required to survive up here in the mountains. Which is better—the beautiful gold filigree of propriety, or the bramble hedge of the wilderness?

Gran chose the wilderness. I chose Lafayette, my own dear Fayt, and he would be a broken man if I tore him from these mountains. What would Etta choose?

-from the journal of Aileana Fay Cook

Etta followed a maid, who couldn't have been more than sixteen, to the third floor of Hazelby House. The girl showed her to a cramped room with a narrow bed, a small chest of drawers, a minuscule washstand and mirror, and a high, round window. Judging by Aunt Rachel's guest rooms in Raleigh, this must have been meant for an upper servant—perhaps a lady's maid—since she'd heard that most servants slept two or more to a room. That she'd been assigned to it was probably an insult, but this tiny, simple space comforted her far more than the grandeur of the lower rooms.

She tried to shoo the maid away, but Beth insisted on staying to help. Or rather, she insisted on staying to do the work in Etta's place, but Etta had no intention of being waited on like an invalid. So she asked questions about Beth's life and the house—like what was the name of the kind footman who rode outrider on the carriage—and distracted the girl from the fact that Etta was putting away most of her things herself.

Beth answered that the footman was Jack. He'd been working for the Sewards since he was ten and going to school part-time. This would be his last year in service, as he'd been accepted to University College in London, where the marquess would provide his tuition when he started in the fall.

Such generosity boded well for Etta's chances of being accepted here, but that was the marquess, not the marchioness. It was the magical members of the family who needed to be impressed.

The act of unpacking and the guileless chatter helped Etta ignore the prickles of excitement and apprehension that sparked over her skin when she thought about what would come next.

Or when she pictured the marchioness's very handsome son. Lady Hazelby clearly had not wanted Lord Malcolm to interact with her more than necessary, and yet he'd ignored the unsubtle hints and showed her kindness anyway.

When he'd first entered the room, he'd filled it with a magical presence so strong and fresh that she'd felt hope for the first time since meeting Lady Hazelby. She'd been relieved to see the distinct silver streak in his hair, and to feel his magic, bright as a summer's day, with hints of cool streams and full of the refreshing flavor of a glass of lemonade.

But as they'd talked, he'd pulled his magic inward, locking it away from her, until he was as contained and controlled as his mother.

She couldn't help the surge of disappointment, then or now. The house was so cold, magically-speaking. At home, her mother would have three or four different spells going all the time, or even a dozen during harvest season when they were always busy. Here, everything they'd done with magic in the mountains was accomplished using machines. They had electric lights strung in the public rooms on the first floor, and water closets on every story. Beth said there was even running water for the baths in the family wing, and dumbwaiters to move food and other items between floors.

Where was all of the magic? She'd passed through a weak ward right outside the house, and there was a stronger ward down a floor and to her right, which she assumed was the family wing. Maybe the marchioness had a private study there, where she did her spells.

How could anyone live like this? Etta's power was untrained, but it was an active part of her—a constant, comforting embrace. It interacted with the world around her, giving her bits of information, and offering more if she opened her Sight. Even now, with her Sight closed, she knew that where this house stood, a Roman couple had once made love in the grass. No one was alive who knew them, but the earth remembered.

She wanted desperately to turn her passive gift into active magic. But there wasn't much active magic to be found in this house. She sighed and thanked Beth, who curtseyed and dashed off to help in the kitchens.

$\sim$

LORD MALCOLM LED ETTA IN TO DINNER THAT NIGHT, AND pressed her, again, to address him informally. Lady Hazelby's cold gaze told her that was not wise, but when the marquess himself told her that they didn't stand on ceremony when it was only family, she agreed, grateful for his support.

For a moment as they walked from the drawing room, she basked in the invigorating touch of Malcolm's magic, delighting in the way it sparkled against her like the bubbly wine Aunt Rachel served at all of her parties in Raleigh. He kept it tightly contained, but where the edges of it rubbed against hers, it sparked with heat, like little matchsticks flaring. Except instead of the bitter reek of sulfur, each brush burst with a bright citrus scent: a mix of lemon, lime, and orange.

Then she got a look at the dining room. The English idea of not standing on ceremony was considerably more formal than hers.

Mal and his father kept up the conversation while Etta stared at her place setting and tried to imagine how anyone could ever need so many items in order to ingest a meal. Even Aunt Rachel's elegant table hadn't been weighed down by so much porcelain, glass, and metal.

The family dining room was—Malcolm informed her—a third of the size of the larger, formal dining room attached to the ballrooms in the back of the house. Considering that this room alone could hold her entire cabin, Etta worried that she would never learn to relax in these grand spaces.

Malcolm seemed to sense her discomfort, because he asked her questions about home. She shared stories of mountain life, grateful for his attentiveness. When he laughed at her anecdotes, she couldn't help staring at his beautiful mouth, and wondering what it might be like to taste him.

A glance at Lady Hazelby chilled her heated imagination, and reminded her of her goals.

The marquess's behavior fell somewhere between his wife's iciness and his son's amiability. He was polite, a little gruff, and genuinely interested in her tales.

"Why did your family stay up there, in the mountains? You say your aunt lived in a city."

"Yes. Aunt Rachel is my father's sister. She married a traveling merchant and went to keep house for him in Raleigh. But my father would never leave the Roan. He could be free there in a way that he couldn't in a city. He belonged on the mountain." Though he'd been dead for years, the wound ripped open—still fresh and raw beneath the scab of time.

She pasted on a bland expression, and made herself continue. "My mother belonged with him, so she kept the cabin, even after his death. She willed the place to me when she died. I sold it to a young family before I left. It will bring them joy, but it held only memories for me."

"We're sorry for your loss, Miss Cook," the marquess said, in a voice that was very like his son's—a rich baritone. Her father had had a clear tenor, and he'd sung in the local choral society as well as around the campfire with his Cherokee kin.

The grief threatened to well up again. She pushed it down deep.

She must stop comparing everything to home, or she would never settle in to this new life.

"Thank you," she said. "I miss them."

Malcolm attempted to change the subject away from something that caused her distress. But as soon as he mentioned a mine in Wales, his father cut him off and started chatting about how a group of American women—all of them married into the *ton*—had recently averted war with the former colonies over some dispute in Venezuela.

"I read about that in the paper at Aunt Rachel's. All of the writers were worried that we'd have another war, when we haven't recovered from our last one."

Lady Hazelby stared, and Etta closed her mouth with a snap. Were women not supposed to have opinions about politics? Aunt Rachel had been proud to have all the latest news. In contrast to Etta's lavish, personable aunt—who never neglected her hostess duties—Lady Hazelby spoke only when necessary and made quelling expressions at her son when he became too effusive.

Not that he paid his mother the slightest bit of attention. The conversation had segued from newspapers to books, and Malcolm made a joke about his father's taste in literature. Etta laughed. Their gazes met, and held, much longer than was proper. His mother noisily cleared her throat.

Etta dropped her spoon with a clatter onto her pudding dish. Lady Hazelby had no intention of letting her son form any attachments. Not that Etta wanted him to form one. She was here to learn magic, not to take a lover. If she must turn that phrase into a repeated chorus in her mind, she would.

After dinner, Lord Giles and Lady Caroline, the Earl and Countess of Abbinden, arrived. Lord Giles was Malcolm's elder brother and the heir to the marquessate. They lived across the square in what was known within the family as

"Heir House." The oldest son traditionally lived there from the time he gained his majority until he inherited.

Malcolm tried to cry off from the evening's engagement, but the rest of the family insisted on his presence at whatever fete or concert they'd planned to attend.

Thwarted, he invited Etta to join them. Her first instinct was to accept and spend more time with him. She'd never known a male mage other than her father and grandfather, and their magic had been specific to hunting and tracking. Malcolm had been trained by some of the greatest sorcerers of the age, including Lilias Fay herself. He would have much to tell her, although he had conspicuously not offered to teach her magic.

One glance at Lady Hazelby told her that her chances of being trained and accepted into the family by the mother were directly proportional to how well she avoided the son. So she feigned a yawn, claimed exhaustion after her travels, and retired to her room.

Beth arrived soon after, but Etta had already undressed and was seated at the little washstand with a rag, cleaning up. With a tsk and a smile, Beth gathered the discarded clothes and said, "I'll take these down to be laundered."

"You don't have to do that."

The maid looked at the dress and undergarments in her hands, and then back at Etta. "Miss, I know it's terrible forward of me, but may I give you some advice?"

Etta nodded emphatically. "I would very much appreciate it."

Beth scooted closer until both of their reflections looked back at them from the oval mirror over the stand. "When my mum was a tweenie, she worked for the Sewards at Hazelby House in Wiltshire. Lord Hazelby's old auntie lived with them, and she were like you, a poor relation. It ain't an easy thing to be."

"I'm figuring that out."

"You need to decide if you want them to treat you like one of them, or like one of us. If you act like one of us, always doing for yourself, and taking on chores, then that's how they'll see you. But if you act like one of them, they'll have to take you on those terms. That's what old Miss Seward did, and she near-ruled the house after Lord Hazelby's mum died. You can do the same. You come from the same blood as Lady Hazelby after all, even if it is awful far back."

Etta laughed.

"And I think Lord Malcolm fancies you. If you play that right, you won't be no poor relation anymore, but a daughter of the house."

Etta's laughter died. "Beth, even if Lord Malcolm fancies me, that isn't why I'm here. I want to learn magic, not get a husband."

"Why can't you do both?" She winked. "I've got to get back to my chores. Think on what I said. I like you. I want them to treat you like a duchess, not like a maid."

"I wouldn't know how to be a duchess. But I'll try for minor nobility."

Beth grinned. "That'll do." She patted Etta's shoulder and bustled away with the laundry.

Etta finished washing and got into bed, replaying the events of the day, from the revelation that Mrs. Upton was actually a titled lady, to the attraction she would have to ignore if she wanted to achieve what she'd set out to do.

Everything had changed the day Ma died, but the changes had seemed bearable in Raleigh. Here, the differences were difficult to ignore. The cavernous halls of a Mayfair mansion might as well be the moon compared with her mother's one-room cabin in what the locals affectionately termed "Fee's Holler." Etta hadn't even known the gap was named after her family until she was old enough to read the true name on a map—Fay's Hollow.

Now she was in Britain, and living in a Fay family house that bore not a single resemblance to her home. The divergence threatened to overwhelm her, so she made her mind a blank, and sought sleep.

THE MOST STRIKING DIFFERENCE BETWEEN MAYFAIR AND FEE'S Holler—and the one she was forced to confront first thing the next morning in the breakfast room—was a tall, charismatic mage with magnetic blue eyes and the same pale-as-alabaster skin as his mother. But where Lady Hazelby's was unblemished white, Malcolm's was liberally freckled by sunlight. He did not—as he explained while they ate coddled eggs and bacon—tan. "I go red as a tomato, and after that peels off I'm as mottled as a brindle hound." When he grinned, tiny lines crinkled the corners of his eyes and mouth. Etta wanted to trace them with her fingertips. Or her tongue.

"You should have seen me earlier this spring, after lambing season. My tenants told me that I had more freckles than sense, but that was fine, because I had quite a few freckles."

Etta smiled at the jest, but once his attention had returned to his food, she gazed at her ungloved hands—the skin brown and the tiny hairs bleached to gold by the sun—and sighed. She had never had a sunburn in her life.

Lady Hazelby entered, her morning gown a sumptuous confection that made Etta's look like a rag on a mountain wash line.

Etta hated the way London made her feel, like the things she had always loved about herself were shameful, or ugly.

She fled the breakfast room, cutting their conversation short. That seemed to be the pattern for the rest of the day. Whenever she encountered Malcolm, they managed to exchange only a few words before another presence intruded. Lord Abbinden dogged his brother's steps for the rest of the morning, and Lady Abbinden spent the early afternoon with Etta, advising her on gowns and deportment.

Late that afternoon, Malcolm managed to come upon her by herself in the music room. Lady Hazelby had still not approached her about a test, and Etta refused to worry herself sick over something she couldn't control. She'd been plucking at the harp strings and amusing herself by trying to reproduce melodies from the gatherings of her childhood.

Since they were, at least for the moment, alone, she asked a question that Lady Hazelby had avoided answering during their last meal. "Why do all of the magic schools in England teach only illusion, or battle magic?"

The abrupt and unlikely question startled Malcolm. His shoulders jerked backward a little, and he stared at her a moment, his eyes fixed on her fingers as she plucked a series of strings.

He eventually joined her at the harp. "The answer is tied up in the history of magic in the empire."

"I know a little, at least what was passed down in the family and what I could read in books. I know about Lilias, dressing as a man to join the army, and forming her group of magicians to fight Napoleon. I know that she was awarded the title Duchess of Fay after Waterloo."

"That's part of the recent history, and it's important. But I'm talking about thousands of years, back to the earliest inhabitants of this little island." He paused, and looked at his hands. They were long-fingered and broad, and not encased in the gloves worn by most of the other gentlemen she'd seen. His eyes were deep blue, and suddenly they were moving again—up from his hands—until his gaze met hers. "Magic runs in families, and magic gives power. So most of the families with strong magic talents ended up with one title or another. They went about the business of acquiring land and property, and eventually they decided that they were done with hard work, and wanted to live a life of indolence and dissipation on the proceeds of their ancestors' labors."

"Indolence and dissipation?" In the mountains, hard work was the difference between life and death. Men who drank to excess or who ignored their responsibilities were reviled, not celebrated.

"Indeed. Now the upper classes flee from public discussions of business and money, unless it's in Parliament when they're fighting to keep more of it for themselves." He gestured off in the direction of the government buildings, to the southeast. "It's become entrenched in the highest reaches of society that 'work' is for the lower classes, or for younger sons who have to make their own way in the world. Any kind of magic that performs a useful function, battle magic notably excluded, falls under that category of work."

"That's ridiculous. Having a purpose and being productive is something for which I strive. I don't avoid it. I want to be useful."

"So do I." Pain filled his expression in a thousand tiny ways, from the slight drawing together of his brows, to the hint of a frown tugging his lips. She wanted to go to him, to kiss those lips until they relaxed and opened under hers. But she couldn't.

"I tried to follow the fashion, for a while." His distress spiked to the point where it radiated from him and into the magical energy of the room. Etta tasted something bitter and sour, then it was gone. He must have shielded himself. She ached for him, for whatever had happened that made him hurt so much.

"Now I don't." His voice was monotone, his mouth a hard line. The next words were cold. "But I think my mother would be happy if I went back to crafting entertaining illusions."

"Why illusion? Didn't your mother learn Lilias's Way?"

"She did, but only because it was the family tradition. Tradition trumps fashion. She doesn't flaunt her skills, though. Most of the time she pretends she doesn't even know the word magic."

Etta opened her mouth to ask another question, about whether or not the middle classes taught practical magic, but Lord Abbinden entered the room and all talk of the arcane ceased.

AMELIA TRACKED DOWN HER QUARRY IN REGENT STREET, at the milliner. Cecily stood near the back of the shop, where the sturdier designs were stored. If Amelia hadn't already known that the Sewards would soon travel to Scotland for Viola's confinement, she would have been able to guess by her choice of hats.

Cecily handed a selection to her maid, who passed it, in turn, to the shop girl. Cecily took care to separate herself from the common rabble, putting on the airs of the haughtiest and starchiest noble matron. It was an act. Amelia remembered Cecily from the days of their come-outs, when they'd spent all of their time together, giggling and gossiping over who would marry whom and, if already married, who was having an affair with whom.

And when they ran out of gossip, they made plans for a future. Together.

But over the course of the Season, Cecily had changed. Roland Seward, the Catch of their year, began courting her, and the ebullient girl, full of humor and magic, slipped away, plastered over by a distant, cold statue of a polite Society Miss. Amelia blamed Cecily's mother, who had no magic and abhorred her daughter's 'dirty gift.'

Now, of course, Cecily had turned herself into the pinnacle of social perfection. She strove every day to prove that one could have both practical magic and good *ton*. Not that Cecily ever cast spells in public. She did not even engage in the prince's fetes, where he held exhibitions and contests for illusion.

Perhaps Amelia was wrong. Perhaps it wasn't an act, anymore. Perhaps Cecily had become the mask.

"Dearest!" Amelia called, and glimpsed the undisguised emotion that filled Cecily's hazel eyes at the sound of her voice. It looked like joy. Then their gazes met and the marchioness's controlled façade was back in place.

Did her pulse race beneath that pretense of stone? Did she remember what they'd once shared? How many spells they'd cast together, and how many times they swore they would never be separated? How the world had been full of promise and infinite potential?

But Cecily had become a statue, and Amelia had become a puppet, with the queen her puppeteer. There were no more possibilities, for either of them. Only the paths they'd chosen.

"Lady Falcestershire." Cecily inclined her head, the correct greeting toward a social inferior. How tedious that she'd managed to snag a marquess when Amelia had only netted an earl. And Cecily's had been young and virile, while Amelia's was elderly and died on her after the first year, leaving her with a title but nothing else.

Amelia bobbed a perfunctory curtsey, for form's sake.

"I'd hoped to run into you soon."

Cecily did not take the bait. Her benign smile made Amelia seethe.

"As I'm sure your new guest told you, we shared the ship from America." Ah, there was a flicker of interest—and wariness. Excellent. "I thought to come to you, as a friend, before it's too late."

"I do not take your meaning." But the smile had become brittle, her hazel eyes too-wide.

"We should not speak of it in a public shop."

Cecily's mouth flattened to a prim line. "You are melodramatic this afternoon." Once, she'd loved Amelia's playacting. They'd done it together, acting out roles from the famous playwrights. Cecily had made such a delicious Romeo to her Juliet. But that was long ago. The marchioness began to turn away.

"It's about Viola." Cecily froze, her body half-twisted toward the door, half toward Amelia.

It was a trump card, one Amelia would not have played had her stubborn darling been more amenable to conversation. But her once-dearest friend's fierce protection of her children was the one bit of true life and feeling still left to her.

Cecily faced Amelia, her hazel gaze unusually heated, the grey and green glittering. "Very well. Where do you propose we go?"

"Let's take a drive. I have my carriage."

Because they would be leaving for Scotland within days, Etta tried to decline any social outings, but when the family met for tea, Malcolm convinced her to attend one of the larger balls that his brother intended to drag him to that night. He argued that she needed to learn about the society she'd entered, and there would be so many people there, no one would notice her.

She'd tried to be good when offered the use of a lady's maid. She'd taken Beth's advice and accepted, although Lady Hazelby's maid, Daphne, scoffed at the sight of Etta's gown. Even by Raleigh's standards, it was not the most elegant. She'd not had time for more elaborate costumes to be prepared, and had accepted this ready-made dress, altered to size. At the time, she'd thought it lovely, and even a little intimidating.

After they arrived at the ball, it became clear why Daphne had sneered, and why Mal had been so certain of his assertions. No one gave her a second glance, except perhaps their hostess, whose eyebrow raised a fraction of an inch when Etta made her curtsey.

Expensive fabrics, heavy embroidery, lace, and ruffles draped every female form across the ballroom. Feathers from a variety of birds adorned their heads, along with more frills, veils, false fruit, and fabric. Etta felt like a hawk beside birds of paradise.

The room itself was enormous. It rivaled the concert hall where her Aunt had taken her in Raleigh, and musicians somewhere in the cavernous space played similar music. She couldn't manage to find the performers. Perhaps they were on one of the balconies, or hidden behind one of the many screens that flanked the room.

The size of the place did nothing to mitigate the closeness of the air, or the smell of a hundred different colognes, perfumes, and bodies. Etta blessed Beth for hunting up a fan, which she now used for its original purpose rather than the fan-language her friend had tried to show her.

She'd heard that London balls always had themes, but this one seemed only to be an homage to opulence. Illusory mythic figures dances along the ceiling, each one draped in a metallic sheen rather than the usual white fabric. Crystal and gold fixtures and ornaments shimmered everywhere. Electric bulbs glared beside glittering magical fairy lights.

Her mother had taught her how to make fairy lights, long ago.

The grief ripped through her, and she had to close her eyes. When she opened them, she had control again.

She distracted herself by watching Malcolm deal with the debs and their mothers. He was always polite, always charming, but never made promises or allowed himself to become entangled with the girls. He never even signed a dance card, yet they all smiled indulgently at him.

Etta wallowed in her anonymity in the corner of the ballroom where Lady Hazelby had deposited her. Once the dancing began, the whirl of color from the ladies and their elaborate dresses was a pleasing diversion from what she refused to think of as loneliness.

Her ball gown—the only one she owned—was a pale gold, cut low in front, with little puff sleeves and a waistline only made possible by a corset that had been constructed for her in Raleigh. It had no beading, embroidery, or lace. The only embellishment was the velvet piping.

She imagined the warm satin glowing under the mixed illumination, pictured herself twirling across the dance floor in Malcolm's arms.

She would probably step on his foot.

A hand brushed Etta's elbow, and even though her skin was protected by a length of soft satin glove, she jerked in surprise at the touch. As she turned, her mind performed the automatic gauge of a person's magical talent that she'd been doing since she was a small child. Most people had only a hint of magic, but Etta had learned to sense even that tiny spark.

The woman had more than a spark. Once she'd turned

enough to see her, Etta realized the woman was also familiar. "Oh!" she said, and then cursed herself because it had come out in the nasal, mountain accent Aunt Rachel had worked so hard to eradicate.

"Hello again," she said, calmer now, and with her accent more firmly in place.

"Good evening. I thought I recognized you. How are you enjoying England so far?" Mrs. Upton—Lady Falcestershire —smiled, her lips a ruby color not to be found naturally on a female's skin. She bore little resemblance to the frumpy woman who'd sat on the deck of the steamship in the evenings. Now she wore jewels and a rich gown of velvet, embroidery, and satin. Compared to her confection of an ensemble, Etta's party dress was downright dowdy.

"I haven't seen much more of it than what we already saw together," Etta admitted. "I drove through a little bit of town yesterday, but it was already dark when we left for the ball tonight."

"I was surprised to see you here. You said you were on your way to England to seek out family connections. How do you know Lady Hazelby?"

Etta paused, uncertain what she should say. She was wary of this witch, although she couldn't decide why. Neither she nor the lady had shared much about themselves on their trip, but they'd spoken several times, and had gotten beyond the polite subjects twice. Still, Etta had always kept the topics light and innocuous. At the station, Lady Hazelby had been cautious, too.

"Lady Falcestershire, how nice to see you." It was Malcolm, free of the debs. He reached out his hand.

"Ah, Lord Malcolm," Lady Falcestershire said, placing her fingers into his grasp. "Miss Cook was telling me that she is staying with your family."

"Miss Cook *is* family." He kissed the air over the tips of

Lady Falcestershire's fingers. "She's an American cousin. Of some remove, but still one of the Fay clan."

"Ah." Lady Falcestershire turned her attention back to Etta. Her gaze was nearly predatory, except that Etta had never thought of herself as prey.

"We met on my journey from America," Etta said to Malcolm. "Our ship sailed from Baltimore, and then we both took the train to London."

"I've always wanted to take a steamship across the Atlantic. Is the current as strong as they say?"

She didn't mistake his meaning. To the non-magical, he would have been speaking of the physical movement of the water. For a magical adept, he could only mean the North Atlantic Drift, an enormous warm water current that circled the Atlantic deocil—clockwise—gathering magical energy as it swirled through the great ocean depths. That same energy was released by the South Equatorial Current, which flowed widdershins—counter-clockwise.

"It was the most powerful source of magical energy I've ever felt," Etta said, and couldn't keep the awe from her voice.

"Only madmen would seek to utilize that source," Lady Falcestershire said, her expression accusatory, as though Etta had confirmed some suspicion about her character or sanity. "No one can control that much power."

Etta frowned. "I realize that. I would never attempt to actually tap the current. But it was a humbling experience to be carried along it."

Malcolm watched Lady Falcestershire with a curious, surprised expression. So he'd found her hostility odd, too.

"I hope to one day share that experience," Malcolm said. "For now, though, I wonder if you will join me in a dance, Miss Cook?"

Etta wasn't certain of the steps, and she did not want to infuriate Lady Hazelby, but she'd have taken any excuse to walk away from Lady Falcestershire. "It would be my pleasure," she said, and accepted Malcolm's outstretched hand.

~

AMELIA ALLOWED HERSELF A HINT OF A SATISFIED SMILE. Cecily had separated Malcolm and Etta from the moment they entered the ballroom, and had established Etta among the wallflowers before being drawn off by a group of chattering mamas.

So, the seeds of their conversation in the carriage had already sprouted. Cecily was clearly suspicious of the American chit, and for good reason. Amelia hadn't even had to lie —much. Marianne Fay's line was tainted, and Etta represented the worst of that rebellious, anarchist spirit.

Amelia might also have suggested that such tendencies posed a threat to Cecily's new grandchildren, not yet born. That was not strictly true, but also not outside the realm of possibility. Cecily hadn't believed the accusation, but she'd been shaken. Her children and her grandchildren were her weakness.

Cecily would be furious that her son had not obeyed her implicit wishes and remained with the 'safe' debs. But Malcolm's desire for the socially-awkward girl served Amelia's ends, too. Anything that put pressure on Cecily to outright refuse Etta's training was worth cultivating.

~

"THAT WAS ODD," MALCOLM SAID AS HE LED ETTA INTO A waltz. She'd practiced this dance only one time, with one of her cousins in Raleigh, and she prayed her feet remembered that single lesson.

"My interactions with her have been decidedly odd ever since we got off the train at Waterloo Station."

He clasped one hand around her back, his silk-covered fingers sliding along her exposed shoulder blade. She shivered, and raised her hand to his shoulder. Their other hands clasped, forming a circle of connection that sparked with desire.

They took their first steps—one-two-three, one-two-three—and Etta grasped at the conversation to distract her from his scent and heat. "On the boat, she said her name was Mrs. Upton."

"It is Upton, just not Mrs." He raised her arm and she twirled under it and out, then danced back to him. He put his arm around her again and said, "She's Amelia Upton, Dowager Countess of Falcestershire."

"Dowager? She doesn't look old enough to be a dowager." Mal's hand dipped lower than was proper, edging toward her waist as they box-stepped. She wanted to push closer than the distance formed by their outstretched arms.

"The earl was quite elderly when they married. His grandson is the earl now, and it's the grandson's wife who is the new countess." He picked her up for a hop, and then set her down again, her golden skirts swirling around them. She wished he would lift her against his chest and then lower her slowly, so that her body rubbed against his.

"I see. I wonder if that's why she didn't use the title with me."

They moved back to position, but this time his hand was firmly on her waist instead of her back. His splayed fingers stroked along her spine. She wished the fancy dress and her corset to the dark god.

"I couldn't say why she obscured it," he said. "To my knowledge, she's a bit of a snob. Which is probably why Queen Victoria chose her to be Queen's Sorceress."

"That makes even less sense. Wouldn't she be proud of that fact?"

Malcolm grinned, and moved behind her, their hands meeting over her shoulders. He stepped close and whispered in her ear, "Maybe she was on a clandestine mission for Queen Vick." The tickle of his breath made every inch of her tingle. Then he stepped back again and they danced with his arm over her shoulder and her arm across his chest. Every point of contact between them pulsed with pleasure.

"Now I know you're teasing me." Etta laughed. She wasn't having any trouble following the steps of the dance. Her body and his moved together with an instinct that aroused dormant needs and made her heart flutter in her chest.

"It's my mission in life to see you smile." His blue eyes crinkled at the corners, and she had to reward him with an answering grin. He twirled her again, so that they were face-to-face, and then the waltz was done.

Malcolm steered her off the dance floor and toward the wall of glass-paned doors that led out to a terrace. The pressure of his hand—still on her waist—made heat flare between her legs. She wanted him to drop that hand to her hip, to pull her hard against his body, and to take her mouth with his.

A booming voice called out, "Seward! Who is this lovely woman?"

Malcolm froze.

A portly man with a bushy grey-and-black beard stood at the edge of the crowd, holding a full glass of spirits. Women in gowns of many brilliant hues and fabrics surrounded him. Etta glanced at Malcolm and caught a tiny frown, quickly masked. He led her over to the man, and bowed his head slightly. Etta bobbed a curtsey.

"None of that, none of that!" the man said. "This is a ball, not m'mother's drawing room."

"Miss Cook," Malcolm said, "allow me to introduce His

Royal Highness, Albert Edward, the Prince of Wales." Etta swallowed a gasp as the crown prince took her hand and defied propriety by actually placing his lips on her glove-clad knuckles. Malcolm continued, "Bertie, may I present Miss Etta Mae Cook, of Bakersville North Carolina." She inclined her head at the prince and gently extricated her hand.

"Well met, Miss Cook, well met!" His Royal Highness, it appeared, preferred to speak in exclamations. Or perhaps that was the effect of intoxication. His cheeks and nose were red with drink, and his words had a bit of a slur. He gestured to one of the women watching from the circle around them, and she came forward. She was in her early forties and wore an exquisitely draped creation of silk sateen, embroidered all over in flowers and vines, with hand-tatted lace peeking out of the neckline. She had a minor magical talent, but one that could be leveraged well if she'd had training. "This is Lady Montbalham. She's from Georgia."

The woman looked down her nose at Etta, which made her feel like the worst sort of pretender in her new gown. It didn't have nearly the panache of the lady's. Aunt Rachel had complained that she ought to go to Paris and have proper gowns done by Worth, but Etta hadn't wanted the expense or the bother. Now she wished she'd taken the time.

"It's lovely to meet you, Lady Montbalham," Etta said, and inclined her head again. Was she supposed to do something more? She wished she could ask Malcolm.

"What brings *you* to London, Miss Cook?" Lady Montbalham asked. Her voice was soft and mellifluous, her vowels the long drawling shape of the Deep South, and no one could miss the emphasis she'd placed on 'you.' As though someone of Etta's background could have no conceivable reason to leave Appalachia. Etta wondered if the lady's family had fled to England after the Civil War. England had been on the side of the Secessionists, after all.

"I'm here to study magic." She didn't add on the honorific address this time. She'd be damned if she'd show any respect in the face of this woman's clear disdain.

"Magic?" the prince asked. "Is that why you're with Mal?"

"Yes," Malcolm answered. "She's a Fay, too."

The prince's entire countenance changed. Despite the muddling of drink, his gaze cleared a bit and focused on Etta, as though truly seeing her for the first time. He had a tiny gift —not much more than the bare spark of magic every human carried within—but he used it now to probe at her. She slapped the attempted spell-net away, as she might a mosquito.

Lady Montbalham gasped, and Etta froze.

She'd assaulted the Prince of Wales with magic.

"Strong," the prince pronounced. "Stronger than Le Fay, I think." He grinned at Etta, then laughed, as though she'd made a hilarious jest. "Once you're trained up a bit, you'll come visit me at Marlborough. I host competitions all season long, and the best mages from the continent come to show their prowess."

"My sister Viola won first prize two seasons running." Malcolm directed his words at Etta and not the others. There was pride in his tone, and love, but something darker, too.

"It was such a shame, what happened to her," Lady Montbalham said, though her malicious tone indicated pleasure, not sympathy, at Viola's misfortune. Malcolm stiffened, tension rolling off of him in such powerful waves that it made Etta twitch.

"What happened?" she asked.

"It's not something I would choose to talk about here," Malcolm said. He drew his magic in, as he had yesterday, and walled everything away. She could barely sense his presence beside her. "Perhaps another time."

At that moment, Lady Abbinden swept up to them. She

greeted the prince, and then hustled Etta off with some excuse about needing her help.

"Steer clear of the prince," Lady Caroline said once they were out of earshot. "His set is...fast. Scandalous. And he likes American girls—a little too much, if the rumors can be believed."

Etta wouldn't hesitate to implement that advice. For all his joviality, she did not like or trust Prince Bertie. He'd presumed to touch her with magic, and then had laughed about it, as though it was his right. And perhaps it was, here in the land he would one day rule. But she wasn't his subject, and she would not be cowed by his lechery or demands.

Lady Abbinden left her alone again with the wallflowers, but Etta embraced the solitude. She no longer wanted to be out under the glittering lights—the shadowy corners were safer. In the space of a ball, she had gathered the interest of the Queen's Sorceress and the Prince of Wales. Pretty much the opposite of Malcolm's pronouncement that no one would notice her.

4

---

*I found myself thinking about Great-Aunt Beatrice for no partic-
ular reason today. Her name flew into my heart on the wind, and
everything smelled of fresh apples, though the orchard is only now
ready for harvest and I haven't brought any into the house yet.*

*I hope she is well. My few correspondences with her have always
been pleasant.*

*Etta got into a fight with one of the neighbor boys this afternoon.
He'd been tormenting a barn cat, and she punched him in the nose.
She's such a little warrior—always so sure of what she wants and
what is right. She gets that from her father. I can't decide if I regret
that she will not follow my path as a healer or not. She is her own
person, and I adore her. But there are so few healers in the world,
and so many skills have been lost. I will be going down to Raleigh
to stay with Fayt's sister Rachel and speak to our congressional
representatives about amending the magic laws to allow for medic-*

*inal magic, but I do not hold out hope for change. The United
States government fears Southern magic too much.*

-from the journal of Aileana Fay Cook

After the ball, Etta drifted from room to room on the first story. She wasn't ready to go to bed, but she couldn't settle on an activity. She wandered into the library, thinking to find a book to read, or perhaps paper and ink to write a letter to Aunt Rachel.

She'd rounded a corner of bookshelves and was hidden from view when a side door opened. A servant—the footman, Jack—exited the smaller, adjoining room, carrying a tray laden with the remnants of what looked like a full supper course. That was likely the marquess's study, since he hadn't gone to the ball and would have eaten at home.

Jack did not close the door again. Etta browsed the selection of books on English history, running her fingers along the warm leather covers, until voices issued from the open doorway.

"Mother, Father, you don't understand. If I go to Scotland —I don't want to—"

"Malcolm." Lady Hazelby's voice was warm, and soft. Etta had never heard that tone from her before, and barely recognized her as the speaker. "You will not hurt your sister or her children, and it is important that all of the family be there. You know why."

"We've had family members miss before."

"Yes, but those were unavoidable situations, and we have always cast the spell again as soon as possible. Clan Fay is only as strong as this bond, Cuthbert Malcolm Seward."

"The magic of it isn't my concern," Lord Hazelby said, "but if your mother thinks it's important, I think it's important. The terms of our deal still stand. Scotland, then back to London for the Season, until you find a wife."

"Yes, and then you'll shower my newly wedded bliss with your financial largesse."

"Don't be sarcastic, Malcolm," his father said. "It's an incentive, not a bribe."

"I don't see any difference." Malcolm was almost shouting now. "And it is not fair of you both to use my tenants, and my financial stability, as a ring through my nose to force me to do something I don't want to do."

"I don't recall parenthood requiring me to sign a contract stating that I would always be fair," Lord Hazelby said. "If your mother says there isn't a risk, you should believe her. She is the strongest and most capable witch in the *ton*."

Even Etta knew that it was uncharacteristic of Malcolm's father to praise magic, so she wasn't surprised to hear Lady Hazelby say, "Roland! I...I don't..."

"Just don't expect me to say it often," he added.

"I hate to interrupt this unusual display of marital affection," Malcolm said, "but I still have a point here."

"No, you don't. Now, run off. I'd like a private word with your mother."

Malcolm made a frustrated noise and must have left through the other door, because Etta heard a click. The marquess and marchioness murmured to each other, barely audible.

She fled the library.

Still restless, and now questioning Malcolm's motives as well as her own, Etta went out to the garden to try and remember what she was doing here. She was only partially successful. Although it soothed her to be surrounded by growing things, the air was a thick haze of coal smoke and fog that obscured even the nearby houses. She could see almost no stars, and the moon wasn't visible from her position. Nothing here connected to the world she'd left.

Even the weight of mankind's presence from ancient times to her current heartbeat did not assuage the sense of detachment and alienation that had settled into her bones. She'd done no magic since her arrival, other than her daily meditations. Lady Hazelby had looked outraged on the way home from the ball when Etta inquired about being tested, and had as much as told her that she was too busy to be bothered.

Malcolm had remained conspicuously silent on the subject, and had yet to do any magic where she could see. Now she knew that he was afraid to be involved in some spell involving his sister and her unborn babes. A man afraid of his own power would not be a good match for her, no matter how much she'd wanted him while they danced.

"Ma," she whispered into the fog, "this can't be what you meant for me. I don't know what I should do."

There came no answer. Not that she had expected one. Her mother's spirit had not lingered on this plane.

No, she had fled as soon as death released her from her flesh, to the Otherlands to find Etta's papa, Lafayette. Aileana and Fayt had shared a deep passion and an abiding love that could never be matched by another. Not even their daughter.

His death when Etta was fourteen had been devastating. Papa had fallen into a gorge, and by the time the rest of his hunting party managed to climb down to him, he'd bled to death from a gash in his thigh.

Etta still remembered her mother screaming at the moment of his death, a keen of agony so sharp that it slashed like an axe blade that had cut her life in two: her childhood with Papa on one side, and her adulthood with Ma on the other.

And now Ma was gone, too, and Etta was alone.

"Are you well?" Malcolm's voice was soft, muffled by the fog and by concern. She ought to have expected him. He turned up in every room she inhabited for more than a few minutes, drawn by this connection between them that neither had acknowledged and that she, at least, had been working hard to ignore. But pleasure still filled her at his presence.

Etta kept her back to him. Not that her features would be visible in this misty darkness anyway. Lanterns on the terrace provided a little illumination, but they didn't do much out here in the winding paths of flowers and shrubbery.

"I'm well enough," she answered.

"That isn't the answer I hoped for," he said. Then, as though emboldened by the dark, his hands descended on her shoulders. Such a touch was forbidden between an unmarried man and woman, and if they were discovered, Etta did not doubt that Lady Hazelby would have her tossed out of the house, all hope of magical training lost forever.

Even so, she did not shrink from the gentle pressure of his fingers. More, she leaned into it, savoring the first comforting human contact she'd been offered in weeks. No, in months. Aunt Rachel was practical and sympathetic, but not affectionate. Etta'd had no true companions on her journey other than the wily Mrs. Upton, and had feared to make friendships here that might endanger her chances with the marchioness.

But despite her need for his tactile reassurance, she didn't intend to bend to Malcolm, or his hopes. He would have to learn that she ruled herself.

"I cannot feel as you might wish, simply because you wish it."

"I only meant to say that I wish you were happier here." He pressed harder into her tense muscles. "A woman who would subjugate her desires and her feelings for a man is not a woman who could hold my interest."

A tiny moan escaped her lips, pleasure from both the touch and his words. He couldn't have manufactured a more perfect answer to meet her objections. And yet, allowing Lady Hazelby's son to caress her was the height of idiocy. She should pull away.

But Lady Hazelby was otherwise occupied, the servants were all about their chores in the house, and the smog obscured them from anyone watching at the windows. She relaxed into his touch, and teased, "What if those desires and feelings clash with yours?"

His breath tickled her ear, and his fingers slid to her collarbones. The gown she wore had a much wider and deeper neckline than any dress she'd ever owned before, and the heat of his hands against her skin—even through his gloves—aroused her. Her pulse tripped and quickened.

He exerted only the slightest of pressures with his fingertips, but that was all it took. She relaxed back, against his chest, and the rest of his body came into contact with hers, belly to back, hips to waist, thighs to hips. She was suddenly very glad that her gown wasn't fashionable enough for a full bustle, just a few extra layers of petticoats in back.

"I don't think our desires are so far apart," he murmured, and her head tilted back to rest against his shoulder. He drew off one of his gloves and skimmed a bare finger up her sternum, to the long column of her throat.

Etta arched her back and the cleft of her bottom came into full contact against his erection. She wasn't a stranger to the male form. She'd been around naked males of every age from the time she first assisted her mother's healing at age seven, and she'd taken her first lover at sixteen.

She knew exactly what she was doing when she pressed back, rubbing her tailbone against him. He groaned.

"Not so very far," she agreed. "Not far at all."

"Gods," he cursed, and bent to kiss her neck. He dragged his tongue over the juncture between jaw and throat, then up her cheek. He woke a fire in her skin and at the core of her body, and then stopped with his mouth nearly tasting hers. "Tell me that you want me." His words were a rasp, his breath scented of after-dinner brandy and a hint of mint trifle. "Tell me that you sense this connection as I do."

She wanted to agree. Wanted to feel his mouth on hers, to taste his lips and his tongue, to turn and throw her arms around him. Wanted him to lay her here in the grass, and strip her bare. Wanted his mouth and hands everywhere, and hers on him. Wanted him inside of her.

Because the need was so great it made her mouth dry, it took a moment to answer. She grabbed desperately at her calm center and found it pulsing and undulating with desire. Great Mother, even her magic wanted him.

This was too much, too fast. There'd never been heat like this with any of her former lovers. A vision of Ma, keening at Papa's death, slammed into her mind. Fear blossomed hot in her chest. This man could take her over, would swallow her with her own desires until she was no longer Etta Mae, but a piece of a bigger whole.

She would not make her mother's choices, would not give up her autonomy and her goals in exchange for a man.

And so she pulled out of his grasp, clamped down on her magic, and said, "Want and desire, even connection, can't justify disregarding my good sense. I need to be trained, and your mother wouldn't want this."

He stared at her, and his washed out features took on the frozen cast of stone. He could have stood in a city square, still and impassive.

Then the stone moved. A tiny shift—a nod of acquiescence. "Very well, Miss Cook." He pivoted and walked back into the house.

~

ETTA FOUND HERSELF ON A TRAIN AGAIN, THIS TIME BOUND for the Scottish Highlands.

She had expected to share a berth in the Pullman sleeper car with the marchioness, but had underestimated the family money. The marchioness had her own, walled-in cabin, and Etta had been allotted an upper berth in the common car, screened off from other passengers by a curtain.

Despite the privacy, she couldn't sleep. She'd been on edge for the last three days, ever since she walked into the door of Hazelby House. Now she couldn't stop thinking about the garden, and the choice she'd made.

She hadn't been wrong, but here in the dark she could allow herself to imagine a world where she could have her magic and Malcolm. No, not Malcolm. Mal. The artificial distance of his full name—or his title—was exactly that. Artificial. She hated artifice, and refused to lie to herself.

Etta slid her own bare fingertip over her collarbone, down her sternum, to the cleft between her breasts. What would it have felt like, if she'd allowed Mal to touch her, to taste her?

Her hand stroked down, into the neckline of her chemise, and over the peak of her already hardened nipple. Would he have been a rough, demanding lover, or gentle and considerate?

Her other hand delved lower, to the place between her legs that her mother had called the clitoris. The mountain boys called it a nubbin, which had always made her giggle. Aunt Rachel, in Raleigh, had called it a woman's pearl. Whatever its name, it was the center of her womanhood, her private source of pleasure and power.

Through the fabric of her chemise, she stroked the tiny, engorged nub. Would he have known to touch her here, or would he have pushed himself inside her, hoping his manhood would be enough to bring her to ecstasy?

She would have taught him how to pleasure her, would have shown him what she wanted, and given him what he wanted in return. She imagined his lips on her slit, and hers on his cock. Pictured him, wet from her mouth, pushing her legs apart and plunging into the heat of her sex.

She dragged up her chemise and thrust two fingers inside of herself, wishing and wanting it to be him. Great Mother, how she wanted him.

Her other hand still played with her nipple. She withdrew her fingers from her tight passage and used the slick wetness to heighten the sensations as she stroked her clitoris. She matched each motion with one at the tip of her breast, and the pleasure finally crested and broke.

She shuddered, still stroking, riding out the climax and the waves that followed, and then sank back against her pillows.

She hadn't made a sound, had barely moved except the strokes of her hands and the little tremors she couldn't control, but she felt as though everyone in the sleeper car knew what she had done.

Etta rolled to her side and punched the pillow. Why should she have to care what others knew or guessed? She'd been taught that her body was a treasure, one that only she could ever own, and that its pleasures and pains were also hers to horde or share as she would.

She refused to feel ashamed. But she did feel fear. Because whether she wanted to or not, she must care what society thought. She needed Lady Hazelby's patronage, needed to learn to use her magic. It was what her mother had wanted. More, it was what *she* wanted.

No more thoughts of bedding Mal. No more fantasies or imaginings. This was real life, not a dream world. He was Lord Cuthbert Malcolm Elliott Seward, and she was Miss Etta Mae Cook.

Wanton, wild Etta Mae could never have a proper English lord.

5

_____

5 March 1886

*Mama and Da are here for an extended visit. Etta is ecstatic. She
loves her grand-da, and he dotes on her extravagantly. Mama
and I went up to the ridge to visit Gran's grave. I had a vision
while we were there of a different mountain, one that overlooked
a large lake, or maybe a bay. I told Mama about it, and she said
it might have been in Scotland, where Great-Grandma Lilias was
born. The mountain was so barren, and yet so green. I will never
see it in life, and not for the first time, I wondered if Gran
missed it. She hated London, but Scotland? If it is as beautiful in
life as in my vision, I could believe she felt a longing for it in
her soul.*

-from the journal of Aileana Fay Cook

Mal looked into the small mirror in his kit and
considered whether he ought to wait until they
disembarked to shave. On the one hand, his
dark hair made the day's growth of beard obvious against his

skin. On the other, the train was doing a fair bit of bumping and he didn't care to lose his head to a straight razor.

He opted against the shave. A bit of beard stubble would not shock the ladies so badly that they fainted across his path. A certain lady would probably find the sight comforting. He doubted mountain men shaved much.

Damn. He had to stop thinking about her. Every time he allowed his mind any latitude at all, it wandered off in her direction. But that way was fraught with problems, not the least of which was Etta herself. She wasn't in England for dalliance or pleasure. She was here to train. He couldn't—wouldn't?—be her teacher. His mother wasn't going to relent, at least not until her fears and worries had been assuaged, and he couldn't ask Etta to choose him over her magic.

So why did he keep imagining her, under him or over him, any way at all, so long as it meant he was buried within her and both of them were gasping and moaning and straining together in mutual release?

Last night, he'd taken himself in hand, right there in the sleeper car with a dozen other men drowsing nearby, separated by a flimsy curtain. But he couldn't help it. The memory of her skin in the garden, of the way she'd pressed against him and he'd fit between the cheeks of her ass—Gods! He'd wanted to push her down, yank up her skirts, and sink into her from behind.

He had imagined doing that as he stroked himself to a quick and violent climax into a handkerchief. And he still wanted it—as evidenced by the rising bulge in his trousers—wanted to feel his seed spill inside of her instead of a damn piece of cloth.

And wasn't that telling? This drive to have a woman—to finish inside of her—was new and strange. He'd always withdrawn before, even when using sheepgut or other sheathes to prevent conception. But with Etta, he wanted everything. Skin to skin, and the chance of a babe. Of many children, binding them together, as he wanted to bind himself to her with vows of a different nature. And perhaps, even…no. Not that. Maybe someday, when she was fully trained, and he could trust that he wouldn't hurt her. Perhaps.

Gods, the fact that he could contemplate using magic again in some distant, hazy future should be terrifying.

Yes, Father, he thought. *I've found the woman I want to marry. Only it's never going to happen.*

Personal obstacles aside, a penniless witch marrying the heir presumptive to a marquessate—after his brother, who'd better produce an heir apparent with haste—would be the talk of the *ton* for the rest of the Season, at least. His father might be willing to marry Mal off to a crofter's daughter, but his mother would never approve.

That was enough to make the pesky erection subside.

After his encounter with Etta in the garden, he'd been furious. She should not have to fear that magical training would be withheld because he was attracted to her. His mother's reticence didn't make sense, and he wasn't the type of person who bent his head and blindly acquiesced to his parents.

No, I'm the type who has to be blackmailed and bludgeoned.

He couldn't be the one to train Etta. He would never go down that path again, not with the calamity that waited at the end. But there was no good reason that he could see why his mother couldn't take her on as a student.

He'd known better than to beard the dragon in her den, or when she still had his father for support, but now was as good a time as any to tell her exactly what he thought. She'd still be in her private car, getting ready, and wouldn't be able to escape.

Her maid was with her, finishing something in her hair,

but the girl squeaked and dropped the comb when Mal barked, "Out, please!"

Mother gave the maid a little nod that she could go, and she did, scurrying off into the corridor. Mal shut the door and let go of his temper.

"What the hell is wrong with Etta?"

His mother arched a single, elegant eyebrow. The rebuke wasn't even aimed directly at him, but at his reflection in the mirror. He could probably have phrased that better, but he was still too upset. He and Etta had been on the edge of something powerful and beautiful in the garden. He'd managed to contain his magic, and she'd been responsive to his touch. Now un-assuaged desire frustrated him, but more than that, he genuinely admired Etta. She had a dry wit, a keen mind, and an experience of the world different from his. There were so many things she could teach them, if only his mother would agree to teach her.

"I don't understand why you withhold training from her." The second attempt was a little better than the first, but his tone was still sharp.

She rose in a fluid motion, something that should have been impossible with the layers of corseting and caging under her dress. If he didn't know better, he'd suspect his mother used glamours to enhance her appearance. She certainly compelled his attention. But such frivolity went against her rigid principles of magic use. "I have my reasons, Malcolm. I know you would rather that I didn't, but I will not take a student without fully considering the outcomes of her training."

He winced. That was a low blow.

"She is an unknown quantity, and we are already in a precarious position with your sister's marriage."

She meant the scandal, not the marriage itself, but he awarded her the second mental point. Both accusations—the

59

scandal and the mishap with a student—could be levied at him.

"If Muireall's school was in London, it would already have been forced to close its doors. Fortunately it is in Scotland. But I will not ask her to take on Etta, either. Miss Cook is a volatile element, and introducing her into the balance that we've maintained since the Lilias's death could be catastrophic for the Fay clan."

"What you're saying is that she's inconvenient, and you're afraid of her."

His mother took another step toward him, and although he'd long ago topped her in height, she still made him feel small. "What I am saying, my son, is that she could be dangerous, even if she does not mean to be. I have been the face of Clan Fay all my adult life. Muireall is too much in Lilias's mold, and she will never be able to move among the *ton* the way I do. I fear that Etta will be worse—growing up in the wilds as she did. How are we to hold up our ideals of magic and attempt to bring public opinion back to our side if we defy convention and are barred from every reputable house and ballroom?"

"You're a marchioness, Mum." He hadn't called her Mum in years, and the childish endearment softened her expression. "There aren't many of those left in the empire. You've been popular since you came out, and now you're a force to be reckoned with in society. If you sponsor Etta, and teach her how to behave, you can both be a bridge back to the kind of magic Lilias believed in."

"I can teach Etta magic." Her voice was soft and almost sad. "But I cannot make her a lady. And she, I think, would not wish to become one."

Mal couldn't argue with that. "Then we need to find a way to make her popular for who she is. Because she is family, however distant. She's part of the Fay clan and she deserves to learn Lilias's Way."

"Your loyalty is commendable, dear, but if I knew how to make unusual things fashionable, I would have already opened a new school for magic in London."

"Why is it so important to bring magic back into fashion? Why not set up a school for the middle and lower classes?"

"Have you not been paying attention, Malcolm? There aren't enough middle and lower class students to teach. Magic isn't only out of fashion in England. It's fading."

Mal stared at his mother. When he made no reply, she gave an exasperated sigh and crossed to a tea service set on a folding table mounted to the wall. The tea was probably cold, but she made a cup anyway. The rote actions calmed her, because when she sat and sipped, most of the irritation had eased on her face.

"When Lilias died, I was there." She stared into the cup, as though scrying for a vision of the past. And perhaps she was. He'd known that she'd been at Lilias's deathbed, but she'd never told him what happened in that room. "She'd asked for me and Muireall, as well as Mother and Aunt Beatrice." She took another sip of the cold tea, which must have been terribly strong as well as cold, because her lips quirked at the taste. She replaced the cup into its saucer with a tiny click of china.

"We'd already been laboring to champion the cause of magic by that point. But Queen Victoria and Prince Albert had done their work well, and practical magic was strictly 'middle class.' The Prince of Wales and his Illusionists were gaining popularity, and I thought to gain favor through them." She put the saucer on the low table in front of her. "Muireall suggested seeking outside of the *ton*, and Lilias gave her blessing to both our endeavors. But she warned us that even by accepting anyone with a gift we wouldn't have much luck. Magic has been fading from England for a long time."

"How long?"

"She didn't know, exactly. Her research pointed to somewhere around the late seventeenth or early eighteenth century, but that period was so full of wars and uprisings that it's hard to tell what is simply magic depletion from battle, and what marks the beginning of the drain of English magic."

"Drain implies it's going somewhere else." He sat beside her on the settee.

His mother allowed him to take her hand in his. "Yes. But we don't know where. Lilias looked for years. And it's so much worse than just less magic available for use. The surface level sources eventually renew themselves. But whatever this is, it's taking the deep magic, the core sources, which means less energy available overall, and fewer and weaker mages born to any mother who lives here during her pregnancy."

"Gods. And no one else has noticed?"

"Why would they? Most of our strong male mages go off to fight wars elsewhere. We haven't had a war on English soil in over a hundred years. Even Napoleon never made it here. And illusion doesn't pull much magical energy from the earth. It's all air and light."

"So you're trying to marshal what mages we have left, to figure out what's going on."

"And to stop it, if we can." She disengaged her hand. "Muireall's handling the practical part of it. I'm the recruiter." She rose, but kept her gaze on him. "So I must hesitate to embrace Etta. I cannot foresee how she will act, but everything she has done since she arrived betrays that she does not appreciate our world. This is not her home, and she has no real ties to our fate. I would choose for her not appear on this stage, rather than pushing in a direction that could lead us all into ruin."

Mal stood, and took her hand again. It was so cold, as though she'd drawn all of her fire and verve too far within her, and all that remained was resignation. "That isn't a good enough reason. You can give her ties. Welcome her into the family, and she'll leap at the chance to help."

"It isn't only the drain that worries me."

"What, then? Make me understand."

"Marianne Fay was…volatile. Destructive. There were good reasons why Lilias did not seek for reconciliation with her, or her descendants." She shifted away from him, her posture turned inward.

"Etta isn't like that."

"How do you know?" Her head came up again, her hazel eyes glittering with frustration. Finally, some heat. "You met her only days ago. Do you believe, because you lust after a woman, that she cannot be treacherous?"

"Of course not, Mother. But it isn't only lust. There's something else there."

"Don't pursue it." She squeezed his hand, hard.

"Why not?"

"Someone I know has foreseen danger around Etta, danger that points to Viola."

"She would never—"

"You cannot know what she would do, Cuthbert Malcolm." She pulled her hand free and stepped away from him. "Even if she has the best of intentions, her magic is untrained, very powerful, and likely wild. I will not unleash that in any city. We will wait until we arrive at Emberlach, where Muireall and I can handle her if necessary."

On that less-than-optimistic note, she left the car.

Mal sighed, and then followed her down the passage, out of her private car, and into the dining car.

A porter seated his mother at a round table with four chairs, and pulled a second chair away for Mal. He sat and they gave their orders. As usual, Mother requested toast and tea, and he requested a full Scottish breakfast, in deference to them having crossed the border overnight. The porter retreated to the kitchen.

"I trust you slept well?" his mother asked, as though their argument hadn't happened.

"As well as could be expected, Mother," he answered.

"I can never truly rest on trains," she said, her tone barely on the polite side of peevish, probably because there were other people in the dining car and she didn't like being addressed informally in company.

The expense of a private cabin ought to guarantee her comfort, but it wasn't for him to judge her expenditures. And Father wouldn't want her sleeping in the common car with the serfs.

He frowned. His mother hadn't invited Etta into her private car. Did she see her as that much less? Or was she so afraid of having connections drawn between them that she wouldn't even offer a more comfortable bed to a distant relative?

As though his thoughts had conjured her, Etta entered the dining car. He took a moment to reflect on certain other thoughts, and his earnest desire to conjure them into reality. That led to another tightening in his groin and some surreptitious movements under the table to adjust matters in his trousers.

At least he had the good fortune to be born at this end of the century rather than the other. A hundred years ago, he'd have been wearing skin-tight breeches with no way at all to conceal his ardent intentions from his mother's keen gaze.

Another porter seated Etta at their table. She requested nearly as much to eat as he had, to his mother's barely concealed disdain. Ladies did not consume mass quantities of food.

Why the sight of her enjoying the food that appeared moments later should arouse him again was a mystery. Perhaps he had a weakness for women who retained their natural appetites. Or he had a weakness for this woman. He certainly longed to be numbered among her appetites.

Eventually it sank in that his mother was, yet again, providing only desultory conversation. Etta seemed to have given up in favor of her breakfast, which was only fair. It was probably a much more fulfilling conversation than what Mother was offering.

But he decided to fill the silence anyway.

"Did you manage to sleep on this jostling monstrosity last night?"

Etta's head jerked upward, and her dark eyes widened a little. Was it his imagination, or did a flush rise under the warm tan of her cheeks?

That was enough to send his imagination down exciting paths, wondering about other parts of her that might flush with heat, with passion, and how he would run his tongue over them and—

"Yes, I did," she said. "Though it took a while to get used to the motion of the car."

"A lady's sleeping habits are not an appropriate topic of conversation," Lady Hazelby said. She didn't look at him, but at Etta. It was meant as a rebuke for them both, but of course she directed it at the uncouth American mountain girl.

"Have you managed to find a window to gaze upon Scotland, now that the sun is up?" he asked instead.

"I did. That's why it took me so long to get here." She grinned as she spoke. It was one of the few true, open expressions he'd seen on her face since that moment of yearning in the foyer when she first arrived.

"Can you feel the magic? It will get stronger, the farther we go into the Highlands."

"I can. It's wonderful. I haven't felt it this strong since I left America, except for the Gyre."

His mother gave him a significant glance, and one corner of his mouth turned down. He didn't want to be reminded of their conversation. What the hell were they supposed to do about a drain on English magic?

"I used to love coming here when I was a boy. Viola and I would play a game where we tried to guess where we were by the sensations of the magic outside the train."

Etta grinned. "I just spoke to the porter, and he told me where we are. What's your guess?"

Mal answered her grin with a challenging smile of his own. He would never do active magic again, but passive magic, sensing and assessing, was no danger and no problem. He opened his Sight.

There was magic everywhere, of course. Mages could draw that power from many sources in their environment, from sunlight to stone. But magic in different places had different properties, and no spell would perform the exact same way when cast in London and again in Glasgow. Usually the changes were minute—barely worth noticing. But the best mages gauged their surroundings and tailored their spell nets to the local strengths and weaknesses. He'd been trained by the best witch of the modern era.

"Maybe fifteen miles outside of Glasgow," he said. "More or less."

Etta clapped her hands together. He'd never seen her look so enthusiastic, or so young. She was only twenty-one, but she carried herself with the weight of far more years. "The porter said twenty miles, but that was a quarter hour ago, so we've probably gone at least five miles."

"Ah, then we've another hour or so to go, as we'll slow

when we approach the city." He pulled his napkin out of his lap and dropped it on his now empty plate. "In Glasgow, we'll join the rest of the Fay clan. Then the lot of us will take another train that will deposit us near Loch Lomond. From there we will ride on a boat, and finally a carriage over some less-than-lovely roads, until we reach Emberlach." He grinned at her crestfallen expression. Obviously she hadn't considered that the train ride might not be the only part of the trip. "We'll stay with the family in Glasgow tonight. If we're lucky, we'll make it to Viola by nightfall tomorrow. If not, we'll have to put up in what passes for a coaching inn there in the wilds."

He gestured out at the rolling green landscape, though the area around Glasgow was hilly and patchworked with fields and farmland. It was nothing like as wild and rugged as the mountains to the north.

If he'd been making the journey alone, he wouldn't have bothered with a carriage, or an inn. He'd have saddled a horse, brought a spare to switch mounts, and ridden at a slow but steady pace through the mountains alone.

It was how he'd always preferred to travel, even above trains. For all their speed, trains were dirty, noisy things. His objections to carriages arose from his boyhood experiences. He'd not much cared for sitting beside his brothers and being berated by a governess for his barely contained energy. Only Viola had been able to distract him on the long journeys between estates and Town. They'd shared their magic and taught each other tricks.

He wished he could do the same with Etta. He couldn't risk it, for a damn good reason. The one time he'd taken an apprentice, it had ended badly. Viola had fixed that, too, and in the end had married the man.

His little sister was nothing if not competent at cleaning up his messes.

Mal's attention returned to Etta. He couldn't think of her as Miss Cook, though he'd never had a problem giving a woman, even his own mother, the proper address within his thoughts before.

Despite her rebuff, they'd had that moment in the garden. They'd been wrapped in fog and in each other's warmth, with his hands and mouth on her throat, and she'd wanted him as much as he wanted her.

So she was Etta in his thoughts, and would be for the rest of his life. He wished they might yet come to familiar enough terms so that he could call her that in private. He hoped, though reason told him hope was foolish, that he would be able to call her that when he was buried inside her.

Another woman entered the dining car. Mal didn't pay any attention at first, but both his mother and Etta stiffened, so he focused on the woman's face. It was the Dowager Countess of Falcestershire. What was she doing on a train to Glasgow?

The porters cleared their meal, and Lady Falcestershire sat at the table beside theirs. Because it would be impolite to ignore her, Lady Hazelby murmured a greeting. Etta and Mal followed the marchioness's example.

"What brings you to Scotland?" Mal asked, skirting propriety. It wasn't precisely forbidden to ask such a question, but good manners dictated that he should have allowed her to address the topic first.

The dowager countess did not seem to mind his impertinence. "Her Majesty has decided to visit Balmoral, and I'm headed that way after I complete some other tasks for her in the Western Highlands."

It would be worse than impolite to attempt to discover the queen's business, so Lady Hazelby forestalled any further questions by making inane comments about the weather and the quality of the food on the train.

When Lady Falcestershire's food arrived, Mal, Etta, and his mother returned to their cars.

∽

Etta sat alone in a window seat of the open ladies car, with a book propped open on her lap but her attention fixed out the window. So far, she'd seen rolling hills and wide stretches of cultivated fields. Not much different from North Carolina. But Malcolm promised that, after Glasgow, there would be rugged peaks and wide lochs.

She had decided to go see how Beth was doing in the servant's car when her magic senses twinged, like spring runoff coursing cold and wild down her spine. She looked up. Lady Falcestershire minced across the car and settled beside her. Etta stiffened.

"At last, we have the chance to speak again without an audience."

After nearly a week of swallowing everything she wanted to say, Etta broke. "I don't know that there's anything for us to speak about, *Mrs. Upton.*"

"Oh, that." She smiled, wide, as though it was a grand joke. "I never use my title when I travel. How gauche! You don't get any sense at all for the realities of the world when everyone is bowing and scraping." She tapped her nose. "And anyway, haven't I asked you to call me Amelia? We're friends, aren't we?"

They weren't friends, but Etta preferred the informality to the title. Amelia's explanation for traveling as a commoner might have been true, but Etta sensed it wasn't the whole truth. "What do you want to talk about that you can't say in front of Lady Hazelby and Lord Malcolm?"

"Why you, of course. And your future."

"My future?" Etta attempted to pull away, but she'd

already been sitting against the window. She had nowhere to go but through the glass and onto a Scottish field.

"I've spoken to Her Majesty about you. She is most intrigued." Amelia smiled as though Etta ought to be flattered by this news, but it made her stomach roil with apprehension.

"Intrigued? By me? Why?"

"You truly don't know?" The lady's little doll's mouth exaggerated the O, and her too-sweet voice turned the question into an exclamation of disbelief.

"Obviously not." Etta pushed her feet against the floor of the train car. But her usual trick of grounding herself didn't work—they were in motion across iron rails. So when Amelia leaned over, her face far too close, Etta's magic was in a frenetic jumble, little sparks jumping out and landing against the sorceress's fluid strength.

"You're a Fay, and you're quite powerful, my dear." Amelia gestured at the place where their magic collided.

Etta opened her Sight so she could actually see the power as it crackled and fizzled into the air. There was a lot of it, but nothing was happening to the excess. It bled off of her and back into the magic currents of the region. She swirled a hand through a snarl of power and it clung, then dissipated. "Power is useless when I can't do anything with it."

"Yes, and the Fays aren't exactly jumping at the chance to teach you, now are they?"

Etta had to agree with that. "Do you mean the queen wants to offer me training?"

Amelia's smile widened. Her resemblance to a china doll wasn't as acute as when her lips were pursed, but her cheeks had that bright, rosy glow. "We want to offer you everything, dearest Etta."

She didn't want to be Amelia's dearest anything, but she

was curious what 'everything' implied. "I don't want to do illusion. Isn't that all the royal family supports?"

"Oh, that's just Bertie and his set. They like their little games and glamours, just like the Fays are obsessed with spells to do things for which we have perfectly good machines. I'm talking about *real* magic."

The door to the private car passage clicked as it opened, and Etta lost her chance to ask what 'real magic' meant.

Lady Hazelby stepped into the public car. Her gaze locked with Amelia's.

Something passed between them. No spells or power, only awareness. But it made Etta hot and cold at once, and the scent of magic in the train car changed from Etta's woodsy, leaf and moss aroma to the smell of wet earth after rain. Etta closed her Sight, and the intense odor was gone, replaced by the leather of the seat, Amelia's perfume, and the ever present coal smoke.

Amelia patted the seat beside her. "Come sit, dear Cecily. We've been discussing my time in America, when I braved the wilds of Boston to find my youngest nephew and his family."

They'd been doing no such thing, but Etta dared not reveal the lie. What if Lady Hazelby decided to send her off to the queen? Mal had already told her that the royals' ideas of magic included the queen's desire for it to fade into obscurity, and her son's ambition to waste it on empty illusions. Amelia had confirmed the latter view, and Etta wasn't sure she could be trusted about the former.

She could not allow that to be her fate. She would convince Lady Hazelby that she was worth teaching, would convince the whole Fay clan if necessary. Etta would not go the rest of her life without magic.

∾

THE TRAIN WAS DELAYED BY DEBRIS ON THE TRACKS, AND MAL risked a social faux pas by going to the ladies car. He asked Etta to take a stroll with him down the length of the train while it sat idle. Lady Falcestershire was there again, chattering at his mother. Etta looked to both women for permission, and Mother shockingly gave it. Perhaps because there were porters and passengers everywhere, or perhaps to get Etta away from Lady Falcestershire.

"Was Lady Falcestershire questioning you again?" Mal asked once they were out of earshot. For some reason, this made her flush.

"Only a little. Your mother had gone off to her private car to freshen up, and before she came back, Lady Falcestershire sat next to me. I don't understand what she wants from me."

"What did she talk about?"

Etta hesitated. "The queen." She shrank into herself a little. "And her trip to Boston."

Mal contemplated that for a moment, pressing back into his seat cushion. He straightened again. "That might be significant. There are Irish in Boston who have only been there for a single generation or sometimes less, since the potato famines. Their ties to their homeland are close, and they have new independence and prosperity in America. The queen fears that Irish Home Rule is coming, even though the most recent bill was defeated in Parliament."

"Would that be so awful?" Etta's people, of course, had demanded independence a hundred years earlier.

"It would, in her eyes. The glorious empire is already crumbling at the edges. Native magics in India have turned back her troops when they attempt to go into the interior. The same is happening in the Far East, and war in South Africa is almost inevitable. The Irish who remain after the devastation of the famines are the ones with the strongest ties to the land, and those tend to be families with magic. You have magic and Irish heritage that's much closer than two hundred years. If you chose, you could be a rallying point for their cause."

"I am sympathetic, but hardly ready to take on such a role. My magic is not strong enough, yet."

"Their mages might train you, you know."

"They might. But it wouldn't be the same." Etta cast a quick glance back down the car to where Mother and Lady Falcestershire chatted. Mal frowned at his mother. She would make an excellent teacher for Etta, if she could unbend a little.

But even now she sat rigid and with exact posture, the façade of perfection never slipping. She'd internalized her role as the face of Clan Fay in the *ton*, and wore that responsibility without fail. Her intentions—to save British magic—were honorable. But he wouldn't want to spend his days making social calls and going to balls and musicales, all to prove that practical magic could be civilized and genteel.

Malcolm had no intention of going back to a society life, much less a life of active magic use. His one attempt at seeking magical fame had ended in disaster. For the last two years, he'd worked to balance the scales he'd tipped so badly.

That had led him into its own kind of trouble with his father and Giles. Father's parting words had been, "Magic can't halt progress. Take a wife, settle her on your estate, and start filling your nursery. Leave the Hazelby lands to Giles and me for now."

For now. Because he was still second-in-line, and needed to make heirs.

Gods, Giles better have a boy soon. Then the pressure would be off of Mal, and he could focus on other ambitions. Like making sure his tenants were all fed and clothed with roofs over their heads this winter.

Etta's desires were more primal. The flame of ambition

inside her was almost visible, strong and hot, seeking something he doubted she could fully express.

If he could help her find it, he would have achieved one of his own desires. Because helping Etta would make him very happy.

What if he *could* help her? Just because his mother chose not to ask Aunt Muireall to train Etta didn't mean he couldn't. Muireall wasn't his actual aunt, of course. She was a cousin of some remove or other. But she was Le Fay—the matriarch of their clan—and she ran the only remaining Fay School for Practical Magic in Britain.

"When we get off the train in Glasgow, I want you to come with me to see someone."

6

31 October 1887

I am lost. I fear to write the words, for if I see them in ink upon the page it will make real what I cannot allow myself to believe. Gran's loss came so hard, so unexpectedly. I have had thirteen years to grieve, and yet the wound is raw and fresh whenever I think of her. How can my heart survive when it is my own parents—

Etta. Fayt. I must live for them.

-from the journal of Aileana Fay Cook

At Glasgow Central Station, they disembarked and took their leave of Lady Falcestershire. Etta braced herself for the mass of humanity and the weight of history, and found both easier to bear here in Scotland.

Mal hired a cab to take them to the Fay School for Practical Magic, and as they drove through the city it was clear that in terms of industrialization, Glasgow was easily a rival to London. She couldn't wait to go into the Highlands, away from coal smoke and the stink of a million people crammed into a single city.

The school filled her with nostalgia for home and left her hopelessly overwhelmed. The glorious sensations of spell-casting, so familiar and so necessary to her soul, made her want to curl up and wallow in the comfortable glow of magic being worked. In one room she felt drenched in cold liquid, could almost see individual droplets beading on her skin. In another, she smelled lightning and all the tiny hairs on her body lifted. Another held the deep, quiet richness of black soil, the tang of metals on her tongue, and the tickle in the back of her mind of growing things.

Magic suffused her again, and it was glorious.

But along with that magic came the people casting the spells. Etta counted at least a dozen family members of all ages between seventy and a babe-in-arms. And then there were the students, who numbered over two hundred. The youngest of those were thirteen, but Mal explained that the school would enroll anyone, even older students who had no prior formal training, so there were middle-aged and elderly students along with the teenagers.

She would never be able to remember the students, but she did try to memorize the names and faces of the many family members who appeared to welcome Mal and Lady Hazelby. The only person she successfully recalled, however, was Muireall Fay Grant, also known as Le Fay.

Mal suggested that Etta be allowed to view a class in progress, and Lady Hazelby reluctantly agreed that she might watch a theory class, but no casting lessons. They were directed to an advanced class that explored the fine line between passive magic and internal magic.

They sat together in the back of a room filled with desks and chairs, but with only ten students in the front two rows. Mal frowned at the empty space.

Etta shared his concern about the lack of students, but was soon involved in the lesson. It pleased her that she could follow the concepts, even if she would hesitate to actually cast any of the spells described. She'd been able to study theory with Ma, who had all of Marianne's books on the subject. She'd simply never had a magic teacher whose spells she could shadowcast.

At the end of the class, rather than take Etta back to his mother, Mal led her to the administrative portion of the building. She saw offices for accounting and enrollment, and finally the Headmistress's suite. Mal opened the door and smiled at the secretary, a young man in his early twenties who had a shock of flaming red hair. In contrast to his vivid hair, his eyes were an indeterminate color, somewhere between brown and grey.

"Hullo, Euan," Mal said. "Is Herself in?"

"She is. She's finishing some paperwork before the trip." Euan tapped at the stacks on his own desk.

"I've got something I'd like to talk to her about."

"Go ahead and knock. If she don' want to be disturbed, she'll tell ye." The wicked smile that accompanied these words indicated that Muireall had no qualms about rousting interlopers from her demesne.

But Mal was right. Who said that she had to wait for Lady Hazelby to make up her mind? Muireall was kin, the same as anyone else in Clan Fay. Etta would still be fulfilling her mother's wishes, and her own desires, if she was trained by Le Fay.

Mal approached the door, but Etta forestalled him. "I should be the one."

"Are you sure? She can be as prickly as a hedgehog."

"I'll take the risk. It's good of you to want to help, but I'm the one requesting the favor. I'll do the actual asking."

Mal subsided, but he wasn't happy about it.

Etta inhaled, drawing air down to her core, where her nerves jangled and anxiety stretched her muscles taut. She exhaled, letting the tension flow away with her breath. Then she knocked.

"Enter!"

The door swung open on its own. Etta belatedly opened her Sight to look for spells. She should get into the habit of checking, now that she was in the company of so many other magic users.

Muireall did not appear at all surprised to see them. "I wondered when you would arrive," she said from a leather-upholstered chair behind a massive dark wood desk. She was a tall and handsome woman, thin but not frail, with hazel-grey eyes and light brown hair. The Fay streak in her hair was wide and shockingly silver at her left temple. She did not quite smile at Etta, but she did not quite frown, either. Her magic felt like the Atlantic Gyre, fluid and deep, with the scent and taste of the salt sea. "I'm pleased you didn't let Malcolm lead."

Etta refused to be intimidated, or flattered. "You know what I would ask."

"Of course I do. But you two neglect to consider the possibility that Cecily and I have had over a month to discuss what to do about you, Etta. We made the decision together to have Cecily lead in this matter. I have my responsibilities here, and I must think of the good of the school. We can't afford to lose it, and enrollment continues to decline."

"Why would teaching me threaten your school?"

Muireall sighed. "That's a better question for Cecily. She understands the *ton* in ways I never will. But I trust her judgment, and she told me to wait. That means you must wait, also."

Shame flooded Etta's face with heat. "I don't want to seem impatient—"

"I sympathize. Truly, I do. By your age, I was already teaching classes here. I respect that you want to learn, that your magic is riding you to be used as much as you want to use it. But you must accept this delay as a necessary evil." She made a gesture, and threads of power ignited at her fingertips, forming a coherent shape. She breathed into the spell and it winked out, gone wherever she'd dispatched it.

"I've summoned Cecily here. Perhaps together we can explain things to you in a way that you can both accept."

Mal approached the desk. "While I've got you alone, Aunt Muireall, I wanted to talk about the blood-unity spell."

Muireall sat back in her chair. "You aren't going to refuse to participate, are you? You hurt Viola enough when you rejected her request to do the marriage binding. It will wound both her and the rest of the family if you deny your place with us out of fear."

"I could injure everyone much worse by being part of it."

"Rubbish. You'll be there, and so will Miss Etta here. All other considerations aside, we can't afford to lose either of your power. Clan Fay needs you both, now more than ever."

Etta wasn't sure what that meant, but Mal seemed to comprehend, because he subsided, though his expression looked thunderous. The magic in the room took on the scent of burnt paper.

The door opened again and Lady Hazelby entered.

"You predicted correctly," Muireall said, waving a hand to indicate Mal and Etta standing in front of her.

"It was not difficult to surmise." She crossed to Muireall's desk, and both women stood behind it. "Malcolm. Miss Cook. I have already explained to you both, at different times, that the decision to train Etta is not easily or lightly made." She stopped a moment, and cast a tiny net of spell-threads. Her hands moved deftly, with quick certainty, until the net had formed. She flicked her fingers and it leapt away from her, hanging in the space between the four of them. "Take the spell."

Etta reached for it, both with her physical hand and her magic. She had no idea what it was for. None of the basic things she'd practiced or read about looked anything like this.

The threads settled against her skin, tendrils of magic wrapping round her fingers. Then it blazed, bright as a star, blinding her with white light and heat, and a pressure like being underwater. The sounds of a gale—wind screaming through rocks and cracks—assaulted her ears. She smelled the metallic-bitter scent of lightning, and tasted something sweet, like clover honey.

The pressure burst with a pop and the spell dispersed.

"Your power is undeniable," Muireall said. "No matter what we choose, to train you or not, your presence will irrevocably change Clan Fay."

Etta blinked away the after images in her vision. Mal stared at her as though he both wanted to run and wanted to gather her close. Muireall wore an eager expression, and Etta remembered her claim that the clan needed her and Mal. Lady Hazelby's expression was a stiff mask, carefully blank, but her hands shook.

"At Emberlach, Muireall and I will test you. We will decide nothing until then."

Mal put a hand on Etta's shoulder. She longed for the contact even as she cursed that she should not encourage him. Muireall would not help them, and Lady Hazelby still held the reins.

After dinner, eaten in the family apartments above the school, Lady Hazelby retired, pulling Etta with her by force of will. Their chambers shared a sitting room, and before the marchioness could disappear, Etta stopped her.

"Lady Hazelby, I must ask. What is it about me that you dislike so much?"

"Dislike?" She gave the word a strong upward lilt, emphasizing the outrageousness of the accusation. "Miss Cook, I do not know you well enough to make such judgments."

"Exactly. I can grasp your reticence to train me. But why avoid me? Shouldn't you be trying to get to know me to be able to make the judgment? And why do you discourage your son from," she hesitated, trying to choose the right word, "courting me?"

Although her posture was already perfectly correct in every respect, Lady Hazelby's back straightened into an even more rigid pose. "You were raised in a world very different from mine, as was made clear in London when you spent more time chatting with your maid than in anything resembling a ladylike pursuit."

"You're right. I don't know how to be a lady." Etta deliberately widened her stance and pushed her shoulders forward, mocking the marchioness's upright posture. "Why does that have anything to do with training me?"

"My reasons would seem incomprehensible and inconsequential to you. But I hope you'll appreciate that they are not inconsequential to me. In fact, they are of some urgency."

"Urgency?" Etta blinked at her and cocked her head to the side. "What could be so urgent?"

"There are many things you do not understand about society, or English magic." Unexpectedly, she gave a little laugh. But it was rue that colored the laugh, not humor. "How could you? You weren't raised inside of it. For now, trust my judgment when I say that you must go slowly. Time will tell. I beg you and my son—do not rush blindly into a situation which could cause irreparable harm to you both."

"Irreparable harm?" Etta's hands lifted and her mouth gaped in disbelief. But Lady Hazelby kept her gaze steady, showing no excess of emotion.

Her reply was simple and absolute. "Yes."

"Do you mean in how people will see us together? How people would see me, the backwoods mountain girl? That's the big problem?"

Lady Hazelby inclined her head in a tiny gesture, as though Etta were a slow pupil who'd finally learned the standard reader lesson. "That should be enough justification for anyone. But I will be honest with you as much as I can. There are other reasons, reasons that are more important than you or me or my son."

"Let me guess. You can't tell me what they are."

"I cannot. There are too many questions to which I do not yet have the answers."

"It's hard for me to accept—"

"You must, and you shall, or you might as well return to America." Her patience was gone, it seemed. But so was Etta's.

"I won't be going back. There's nothing for me there, except memories."

"Then you'll abide by my will, if it is your choice to remain here."

"It doesn't seem I have a whole lot of choices left, but yes, I will. But I can't speak for him."

"No, of course you can't." Lady Hazelby seemed truly shocked that she would make such an assumption. "I will not hold you to blame for his actions. I'm not that cruel."

"Thank you for that, at least."

The marchioness gave a tight nod of acknowledgment. "Rest now. There is still a long and bumpy journey ahead of us tomorrow."

That touch of humor gave Etta hope. Lady Hazelby hadn't

relaxed at all in Etta's presence since she first met her on the train platform. The woman still had reservations, but there was a chance her icy demeanor would eventually thaw.

Etta refused Beth's help, and dressed for bed alone. But she couldn't sleep, and so she laced her sturdy boots, drew on her pelisse, and took a candle back downstairs. Seeing the world by lantern and candlelight again had made her long for home.

In London, the townhouse had been wired for electricity in the main rooms. The guest chambers and servant's quarters still had gaslight, but even that had an alien quality, both steadier and cooler, with less smoke, than flame produced by candles or oil.

The electric light had been preternaturally bright—a steady brilliance over every surface. With no comforting dark corners, Hazelby House left her unsettled.

The school had gas lamps in the classrooms and public areas, but the dorms and guest rooms had not been converted. Now, while the school's denizens slept, shadows abounded. She crept down the back stairs into the kitchen. There were gas lamps here, too, but only a few of the sconces were lit, and the flames were low.

The door into the back garden was unlatched, which should have struck her as odd but didn't until she was already through it and exhaling wisps of condensation into the night air.

It wasn't as bad here as in London, but it was still a city. The sky was obscured by clouds, and there were noises from the buildings nearby. Etta imagined patrons in pubs, mothers with young children, workers heading out for late shifts in the factories. She would find no stillness here, but perhaps she could seek a different sort of magic.

With her second breath, she sensed him. Of course he would be here. Lady Hazelby had magic but preferred to forget it, even the passive knowledge of its power. She would not seek communion with the world spirit, or with the energy of so many living beings in one place. Malcolm might eschew active magic, but he longed for what he had forsaken.

Ma had taught her all life is connected. Every stone and star, every breeze and tree, from the water that gives life, to the earth where all will one day return.

Etta had thought she understood the concept—had felt herself enmeshed and entwined with the universe. But she hadn't comprehended that she could feel this deep sense of sameness and difference, of codependence and interdependence, with another person.

Malcolm Seward made her part of a different whole.

She feared that connection and, at the same time, desired it.

She went to him where he stood on the far side of the courtyard, near the gate in the stone wall that let out into the alley behind the school. A gas lantern on the wall turned him into a dark silhouette. Despite her promise to Lady Hazelby, his presence there, alone, was too much temptation. She wouldn't push—wouldn't seek his passion—but neither could she deny him, or her, the sense of completion, of rightness, that connected them. The Cherokee saw the world as a sphere and the People as guardians and protectors of that sphere, maintaining harmony through equilibrium.

When her bare fingertips slid into his palm and he grasped her hand tight, many things came into balance. Future and past, magic and mundane, sorrow and joy.

They stood like that for a long time, separate beings welded together by twined fingers. Etta's magic rose and quested outward from the center of her being, flowing toward that point of connection, meeting his where it did the same. And then their minds and hearts meshed as their bodies desperately wished to do.

Etta gasped. She'd never experienced this kind of merging before. She and her mother hadn't melded their magic because their talents weren't compatible in the slightest. Ma had done what she could, but her magic was wild. Not in the sense of being uncontrolled, but as part of the wilderness. Aileana was a creature born of Scots-Irish Faery and Choctaw nature spirits. Etta could no more merge with that wild nature than she could with a non-magical person.

Mal's magic was energetic and feisty, but not wild. His motion and her still, strong core came together like a crank-shaft fitting into a gear. Sparks and heat erupted inside of her, a mix of desire and exultation.

Her mother had once tried to explain how sex could be used as a source of energy for magic. Etta hadn't understood. None of her earlier sexual partners had made her light up this way. Perhaps, none had ever truly touched the core of her, her secret self.

She'd never wanted anyone to. She'd seen where that kind of sharing led—to choices that took her mother away from her family and up a mountain. Choices that left them both alone.

If Mal could make her feel this way from linking their hands, what would happen if she kissed him? If they slept together? Great Mother, she would be lost.

Etta wrenched her hand out of Mal's. Her magic refused to be disengaged so easily, and the effort made her sweat. She yanked harder and something tore, the seam holding their magic together ripping open and leaving threads of power dangling in a knotted mess.

She gasped with pain at the abrupt freedom.

"What the hells?" Mal cried. He lowered his head and raised his fingers to massage his temples. "Gods, that hurt."

"I'm sorry. I don't know what I'm doing." Her own head

throbbed, from the back of her neck all the way around to her jaw.

"That's pretty obvious. Shite." He groaned and rubbed harder.

She lifted her hands toward him, and he backed away.

"Not a good idea. My magic is primed for self defense, and I can't speak for what would happen."

Etta took her own step backward. She'd never considered teaching herself magical defense. Who would she defend against?

"What does that mean, exactly?"

"It means that all boys who have magical talent go through military aptitude training at school." He dropped his hands and their gazes met. "I was apt." For a moment, something cold and dark shone out from his blue eyes.

Etta shuddered.

Then one corner of his mouth tilted up and the glitter turned from danger to humor. "Aye, I could have been a battle mage, except for the tiny little problem that I didn't like fighting. Still, some habits are hard to break."

"So what do you do instead of fighting?"

"Nothing." His good humor soured a little. He disliked idleness, as she did. Their gazes met, and his eyes narrowed a bit, as though he were trying to decide something. He shook his head in a tiny, negative gesture, and said, "I tried to institute some improvements at a mine my family owns in Wales, but no one was interested in progress, not even the people who would have benefited from my work."

It was an evasion, a half-truth, but she didn't press him. Instead, she pursued the topic he'd introduced. "Miners are a tough people, and set in their ways. It was the same at home." She rubbed the back of her head. The ache had subsided, but had not yet dissipated.

"So it's a hopeless cause?"

"I don't know enough about mining to be specific." She pulled the ribbon out of her hair so that the long strands would fall loosely down her back. That helped relieve the remaining tension. "But from what Ma told me about trying to teach the mountain people hygiene and medicine, I would say that you need to find a different way to present your ideas. Make it seem like they thought of it, or figure out how what you want to do can be integrated with what they already do. And give it time. They move at the pace of the mountains: slow and steady. Like a mountain, they won't move just because you ask. They have to choose."

"Time is something I don't have much of these days."

"Why is that?"

"My father expects me back in London after Viola gives birth. I'm to be paraded about on the marriage mart as husband material."

Something stilled inside of Etta. She remembered the conversation in his father's study, which she'd successfully managed to ignore until now. His family wanted him to get married. Was that his reason for pursuing her?

He didn't sound happy, but families could be persuasive. Mal was the sort to walk away if he didn't have a good reason to follow his father's commands. What was his reason?

She shouldn't ask, and yet she could not keep the query inside. "Do you have to do what he says?"

"That's a deceptive question. Of course I don't *have* to do anything. But he's threatened to cut me off from my allowance and not cover my expenses. I would still tell him to go hang, and figure out my own way, except that I recently purchased a property in Scotland to save the tenants from being turfed out in favor of sheep, and they're depending on me. All of my capital is invested in making much-needed repairs to the crofts, the village, and the fields. I mortgaged the house to buy seed and livestock, and I've been repaying the loan with my allowance."

"So if you lose your source of income, you'll have to sell the estate?"

"Not right away, but it would come to that sooner than I'd like." He ran a hand through his short-cropped dark hair. The light of the lantern hanging by the gate gave it a slightly reddish cast, especially the silver Fay streak, and his pale skin glowed gold. She wanted to touch him, wanted to lean in close and smell that delicious mix of soap and starch and musk, wanted to lick the salt from his skin and feel his tongue tangle with hers.

But that way lay obsession, and the arousal of desires best left chained.

"I'm sorry you're being forced to marry. My mother made many of my choices for me before I understood what those choices might mean, but she never forced me to make such a permanent decision."

"Welcome to the aristocracy. Wed for money, position, and obligation, and no one cares if you like each other or have even the smallest hope of getting along. Most of my school friends who have married spend their days completely separated from their wives. I don't ask, but I assume they only consummate their marriages infrequently and for the purpose of conceiving an heir. That's certainly what my father wants."

"He wants you to marry a woman you will only encounter a few times a month in a darkened room, completely clothed under the bedsheets?"

Mal laughed. "Well, that's not entirely fair. What I meant was that he wants an heir, but I'm sure he'd like me to be happy, too, as he is with Mother. The gods only know how they manage it, but they actually seem to have some sort of respect and even affection for each other." He frowned. "I want more than that."

Etta looked away, toward the dark, cloudy sky. She couldn't see him and not want more than that, too. She steeled herself, and said, "There are reasons to desire that kind of relationship. Your parents use their heads, and make decisions based on logic and reason." Her fingers clutched at her robe. "My parents were obsessed with each other. They followed their hearts and made mad choices in the heat of passion. I don't want that for me, or for my children."

Mal approached her, and the hairs on her neck rose as if they could reach out and caress him. His breath moved against her ear, but he did not touch her otherwise. "Is there no middle path? No way between my parents' ice and your parents' fire?"

She kept her back to him, because fire was what raced along her skin and through her veins when he came near. "I don't know. But right now, I can't afford to find out."

He made a non-committal sound, and backed away. With more distance between them, she felt safe to face him again. He stood silent, the light of the lantern exaggerating the planes of his features, the sharpness of his cheekbones. She longed to reach for him, but the very strength of that longing stayed her hand. "I wish you good luck, finding a woman who can take that path with you."

His expression shuttered, and he became once again the statue of a man he'd been in the London garden. He bowed his head to her, acknowledging the distance she'd enforced. "There's only one woman who has ever inspired me to try. I have no intention of looking for someone to be second best." He put his fingers to his lips and then turned his palm out so that the kiss faced her, each gesture deliberate. "Good night, Etta Mae."

Mal strode back inside, but Etta remained in the dark

courtyard. Passion and logic and magic warred inside of her. Mal wanted her. Etta wanted Mal, but feared him, too. Choosing him meant sacrificing magic—meant succumbing to the flames of desire.

They would burn her to ashes.

7

19 December 1887

Great-Aunt Beatrice is dead. I received a curt letter from someone named Lady Cecily Seward, Marchioness of Hazelby, grand-daughter of Her Grace, Horatia York, second Duchess of Fay. I'm quite sure she thinks of herself using her entire title, all of the time. Apparently Beatrice became the third Duchess of Fay in 1885. I'm surprised she didn't write me at the time. She told me, when her sister became duchess, that she would not be writing again. Horatia hated her youngest sister, and did not approve of anyone contacting Marianne's—Gran's—heirs.

Why not send word after Horatia died? I can only speculate. But this Cecily must take after her grandmother. She obviously wrote only out of a sense of familial duty, because she saw my name and direction in Beatrice's correspondence. She did not say who had succeeded to the title. I don't even understand how it passed to Beatrice instead of one of Horatia's children. Would it have gone to Gran, if she lived?

Traveling with the entire Fay clan was a chaotic experience, but as Mal watched, Etta remained focused out the carriage window, hardly reacting to the bustle and noise of the rest of the passengers, riders, and carriages. She'd been cordial to his two cousins when they claimed the opposite seats in their carriage that morning, but the girls wanted to talk about boys and school gossip, and Etta had little to offer to their conversation.

What did she see out the window? Did she feel the same soul-deep draw to the land as he did, whenever he came home?

London had never been home to him, not even as a child. Nor had the Seward estate in Hazelby, near Swindon. Though fertile, the flat English farmland held no appeal for his magic soul.

If what Mother and Aunt Muireall said was true, that might be because the drain of English magic was concentrated in the southeast. Scotland was in the northernmost region of the isle, and still held most of its magical essence. Of course his connection would be stronger to a place where magic gushed like water along a Highland burn in spring, swollen and surging with snow melt.

Last night he'd gone in search of that bond to the earth, and had found a different kind of union with Etta and her magic. When she'd broken that tie, he'd reeled, not only from the pain, but from how deep that connection had gone.

He'd merged his magic before, of course. First with Viola, who had a knack for linking, and later with his instructors at Harrow. But those had always been surface links—magic only—or sometimes the public level of the other person's consciousness.

With Etta, he'd delved straight to her core, and had

opened his for her. Never had he experienced such bliss, such absolute joy. But then something changed. She went from brilliant heat to a shard of ice, and severed the connection.

Was it only his mother's objections that held her back? Or this thing she believed about marriage—that to have passion was to lose one's self?

Hadn't she felt what he did? When they'd come together, he'd felt more himself, more truly alive and individual, than he'd ever been apart from her. She complemented him, her fixed earth grounding his mutable water and flame, at the same time as he showed her how to flow and burn.

As long as they did not attempt to cast any spells together, he wanted to experience that connection again.

The carriages were twice mired in mud, so the clan decamped at an inn late that evening. The High King's Arms was the only place on the main road through the Highlands from Loch Lomond to Glencoe that had enough rooms to accommodate them, and they'd been lucky to arrive before dark, even though the midsummer sun took its time falling behind the mountains.

Everyone was cranky and hungry, and sought their suppers, but Etta managed to slip away from the group. She went out through the inn's yard and onto a worn dirt path that Mal knew well from many years stopping over at this inn. He followed her.

She stopped at the river, though the path continued over a footbridge and up the slope beyond. The setting sun illuminated her from behind, revealing a secret fire within her dark tresses. He stayed several feet away, wondering if she'd acknowledge him, or not.

When she spoke, it was to the river, with her back still turned to him.

"I'm sorry again for last night. I had so much confidence after sitting in on that class. I knew or could understand everything they talked about. But practice is quite different from theory."

"Don't be so hard on yourself. Linking is hard for anyone the first time, and it isn't usually so...intense."

She twisted then, and looked over her shoulder. "So that wasn't...usual?"

"No." He took a few steps closer and held out his hand. This, he could give her. "Let me show you how it's typically done."

She hesitated, and stared at him. He thought she would demure, but she took a deep breath, pivoted, and placed her hand in his.

When their skin touched, some of his bravado fled. Doubt crept back in. He oughtn't do this. The last time he'd tried to train someone...

No. This wasn't true training. They would do no spells, would only merge their gifts. And since he very much wanted to touch Etta, he needed her not to fear what would happen when he did.

"I'm going to initiate the link. Don't do anything, and don't fight me. I promise I won't push."

As it had before, their magic joined with breathless ease. But this time, he did not give in to the temptation to take the connection deep. He held back, touching only the outermost portions of her conscious mind.

There. That's not so bad, is it? he said into her mind.

Her eyes widened in startled amazement, and her fingers clenched his. "I'm sorry," he said aloud. "I should have told you about that before I did it."

"Strange," she said. "When you spoke, I heard the echoes in my head."

"It's like that for me, too." He switched to his mental voice. *That's why, when sorcerers link, they tend to speak mind-*

to-mind. Otherwise, it's like standing at the edge of a crevasse and shouting into space.

How odd. But I realize why Ma would never try this with me. Your magic is the same as mine in a way hers wasn't. A connection between her and me would not have been stable.

This isn't precisely stable, either.

Fear spiked through the bond. *What do you mean?*

Don't worry. I'm controlling it. He squeezed her hand. *Last night, you initiated the link, and you didn't know how to stop your magic or mine from doing whatever it wanted. But I won't let the tie go any deeper than this.*

Relief, and then something else. Something hot that made his cock twitch and his mouth water, before it was suppressed from her conscious mind.

That was probably for the best. *I'm going to break the link now, but keep your hand.*

She nodded, and he gently released her magic. "You were right," she said. "That wasn't so bad. Thank you."

"You're welcome. But don't try to initiate any more links until you've had a good bit more practice. If you want to link with me again, allow me to lead."

"I will." She looked back out over the water. "Can you tell me what I should expect? With your family, I mean."

"They're your family, too, distant and extended though they may be."

"Yes, well, right now they are strangers, and I don't know what to do around them. I never had to worry about what I said in the mountains at home. Everyone knew me and Ma, and they respected us. I didn't have to worry that if I said the wrong thing, I'd be snubbed at parties."

"Were there no social consequences, then?"

"Oh, there were. But Ma was the healer, and for many of them, something just shy of a deity. They called her the Wise

Woman of Fee's Holler, and if she told them to do something, they did it."

"Even if it went against longstanding beliefs?"

Etta gave him an odd look, one eyebrow lowered. But then her expression relaxed. "I forgot I told you about that. She did have trouble when I was little, getting them to accept her. But by the time she died, she was so much a part of mountain life that everyone looked to her for answers and advice, even about non-medical matters."

"She sounds like one of the fairy healers, in the days before they left the world of men and returned to their lands beyond the Sea."

"I always thought of her as a mix of Choctaw nature spirit and Gaelic Faerie." Etta laughed. "Would you tell me a story of the fairy healers, so I can hear how she was like them?"

"I will, if you'll walk with me a while." He lifted their linked hands and placed a kiss on her knuckles. Then he dropped the hand and offered his elbow.

She ignored the elbow and used both hands to lift her skirts in preparation for a hike. He chuckled, and led the way. They set off across the footbridge, and his laughter changed to tales of times past, of fairies and warriors and legends.

THE HIGHLANDS WERE GORGEOUS. ETTA HAD FEW COHERENT words to describe the scenery other than synonyms for the same. Her own mountains were tree covered, full of creatures both prey and predator, and their forested slopes hid secrets in the sun-dappled shadows.

In this land, grass and rock stood naked and alone beneath the oft-cloudy sky, a barren loveliness that was ancient and strong. Yet Mal spoke of secrets, even here. Of moors where whole clans of men could disappear into the heather.

He spoke, too, of their shared family, of the Clan Fay of old. Of their ancestral home on Skye, and the dramatic rise of Lilias, from gentry to a duchess, and the slow decline during the long years of Victoria's reign, a decline that began when Marianne Fay, Etta's great-grandmother, ran away to marry an Irishman.

Now that she'd learned more of the English side of the family history, Etta understood why Lady Hazelby treated her like a destroyer of worlds. In some ways, she represented the independent spirit and willful disobedience that had long categorized her family in America.

The sun sank behind the mountains, and the sky darkened to dusk.

"We ought to get back to the inn," she said.

"We will. I want you to see something first."

He'd led her to a little hillock, topped with a tiny ring of stones. These were not giant menhirs, like the famous stones on Salisbury Plain, although the central stone was nearly as tall as Mal and thinner than the others. Most of the boulders were less than four feet tall, squat and round, carved all over in ogham tree script and runes.

The light had faded, the sky gone inky and black, but the stones were as visible as if the sun shone overhead. Mal brought her into the circle, to the slender stone in the middle. Designs flowed across the surface of the rock, carvings that mimicked air, and flame, and water.

Mal lifted his arm and held it out, stopping short of actually touching. She took the hint, and placed her palm against the megalith.

Power leapt from the earth and shot through her body. The carvings glowed with brilliant colors, a panoply of light and motion.

Mal spoke, low into her ear, on the other side of her body from where he'd been. "Scotland says hello."

The magic pulsed along her veins, filling her with so much heat that her skin must be glowing like the carvings. Without breaking her hand's contact to the stone, she turned and looked at Mal. They now stood face-to-face, and he watched her as though he were in awe.

Awe was far too tame a word to describe it. "I've never felt anything like this."

He placed his hand over hers, and the power expanded, drawing him into the circle of magic. But Mal never looked anywhere but at her face. "Neither have I."

She raised her free hand and touched his cheek.

He didn't say anything else, but some gravity or magnetism pulled them together, until they were wrapped in each other's arms, seeing clearly in the light of Scottish stones what had been obscured in the London fog.

Everything she was yearned to take the connection deeper, to explore that new world she'd only briefly glimpsed before. She wanted this man, wanted his honesty and his tenderness, his humor and his strength. Wanted to know the taste of his mouth and the softness of his skin. And so she prayed his mother would forgive her, and pressed her lips to his. Something of her soul fled along with her breath into him, was exchanged with a piece of his. Their mouths opened and their tongues stroked and pressed, seeking a more intense bond, seeking a way inside each other.

*I need...*her thoughts, echoed by his, *I want...*

Then it became, *we need, we want*, and their hands moved along each other's bodies with an aching urgency. His fingers delved under her pelisse and against the bulky skirts of her traveling dress. Thank the gods it was made for comfort, to be worn without a bustle or corset while riding in a carriage. He molded the fabric against her waist and hips, then down to her ass, pressing her into him so that the ridge of his erection stroked her belly. She slid her hands up his back and down again, cupping his ass as she rubbed herself against him.

His fingers quested upward, finding her breasts, the nipples peaked and hard beneath the cotton of her shirtwaist. He stroked and she gasped, arching into his hands. She cupped his erect length in one hand, stroking it, and then dropped to her knees and pushed him back against the stone. She undid the buttons on his split fall and he gasped when the cold night air touched his skin.

Etta smiled and replaced the chilled air with the warmth and moisture of her mouth. Mal groaned and made a little, unconscious thrust forward, the hard length of him sliding between her lips and deeper into her mouth. She ran her tongue along him, lapping at the exposed and sensitive head. She reveled in every gasp and moan, slipping her lips over him, stroking the heavy sac beneath his shaft that was now drawn taut with arousal.

He pushed her away, roughly, and tugged at her shoulders until she stood. Reversing their positions, he pinned her back against the stone. The rock face nearly pulsed with heat and light, shining on his face as he ravaged her mouth with his. She met the thrust of his tongue, glorying in the touch of his hands once again on her body.

Mal hiked her skirt up to her thighs. A brisk breeze flowed over parts heated by desire, and she broke their kiss to hiss a shocked exhalation. He slid down her body and disappeared under her skirt. She leaned back against the hot, vibrating stone as his fingers stroked over her stockings, past her bare inner thighs, to the slit in her drawers, teasing ever closer to the sensitive skin of her core.

Then it was not his fingertips but his mouth that found her, his tongue darting unerringly into the top of her sex and laving the foreskin of her clitoris, again and again, swiftly and with enough pressure that she came, crying out into the dark. He did not relent when she began to buck and mewl against his mouth, but drove her higher, pressing the orgasm to a climax unlike any she'd ever experienced.

After the shocks receded, he stood, and she sagged against him.

On the edges of her bliss, something tickled at her mind, some reminder of reality and tomorrow. But the magic of the stones, and of Mal, throbbed all around her, and every beat of her pounding heart wanted nothing but to be held here, forever.

The moon had risen while they dallied, its shape just past half-full, and its cool light, mixed with the magical illumination of the megaliths and the twinkling brilliance of the stars, gave Mal's skin a pearlescent and unworldly glow. But he was of this world, and—at least for this moment —hers.

I would give you release, she said into his mind, where they were still tangled together.

I've already found it through you, he answered. *And I want the first time to be inside you, truly. Not your mouth, but deep in your womb.*

She turned her startled gaze to his. "What of children?" she said aloud. She had ways to prevent conception given to her by her Choctaw and Cherokee kin, but the English would not know much of native ways.

"I'd welcome a child created between us." He held her tight. Oddly, there was no internal echo. Almost as though his physical and mental voices were perfectly matched within her. "And I'm willing to wait until you feel the same."

She scoffed. That was some presumption. "If I never do?"

He smiled, and pressed his forehead to hers. "You forget I'm already inside your head, love. I can sense the need in you, as it is in me. You long for a family of your own. Your mind isn't ready, and so I'll wait. But your heart yearns."

Her hands clutched around his back. "You can tell so much?" She didn't want the fear, didn't want to let it taint what they'd found, but it crept up, showing her every crack in the once-solid walls of her heart. What would happen if they all shattered?

Mal kissed her forehead and stroked her hair, cradling her against his chest. "You can, too, if you want. I've never gone this deep with anyone else before." His joy at their connection soothed some of her worries. She followed his suggestion, peering inside of him. His need to complete what they'd started was sharp and keen as a blade. Deeper, she sensed a raw ache for a family of his own. An ache so like hers that more of the fear receded.

"There are ways to prevent a babe from beginning. I do not wish for a child, yet, but I do wish for you to be inside of me."

He groaned and kissed her. "Gods, I want that, too." He pulled back. "But the reasons you've rebuffed me before still hold true. Mother doesn't want us together, and I don't want her to have any reason to deny you training. I'd teach you myself, if I could, but..."

"And why can't you? Or your sister, on her own? I appreciate Muireall's reasons. She has to think of her school. But why not you? Does your mother get to decide what you two do with your magic?"

"No. It isn't my mother's decision." Mal closed his eyes, tensing himself against whatever answer he was about to give. "Four years ago, I took an apprentice. I was here, in Scotland, at Emberlach. It's my mother's estate, which she brought to her marriage with my father, and we came here often growing up. Ian was our neighbor, and had a good, middling talent. We'd seen each other often as boys, but his father had sent him to Radley instead of Harrow because Radley doesn't teach magic. He didn't want a mage as a son." Mal's shoulders hunched inward. Etta twined her arms up around his neck.

"We both thought we were men, grown up enough to make our own decisions. So I decided to train him. He was nineteen and I was twenty-one. We worked together for over two years, and then I nearly burned the magic right out of him. He sought to keep up with me, to do as I did, and I never realized that, instead of pushing him toward his potential, I was pushing him past his limits."

Etta squeezed him, wishing her touch would be some comfort. "What happened?"

"We were in London, for the season. We'd fallen in with the Marlborough House Set." Her quizzical expression must have informed him that the name meant nothing to her, so he clarified. "The Prince of Wales lives at Marlborough House. Well, sometimes he does. More often he visits other people's estates so he can drain all of their funds instead of his own. Anyway, his friends and cronies go by that name. And for a while Ian and I sought their acclaim."

He settled back against the stone, but his muscles still bunched with tension. "Ian decided to throw a party for the prince. It was the fashion at the time—as it still is, I suppose —to have spectacular magical entertainments at balls and fetes, especially when Bertie was invited. Every party had to outdo the last. Such a frivolous waste of our gifts. And more than Ian could handle."

Malcolm shuddered, and Etta wrapped her arms around his waist. Their magic was still intertwined, and his shame and self-disgust washed over her in waves of alternating heat and chill. His voice cracked, and Etta's stomach clenched in sympathetic queasiness. A sharp tang, like spoiled lemons, filled her nostrils. Mal's usually citrus-bright magic had turned inward, and she understood why he feared to use it like this.

"We were building the grand illusion that was to be the highlight of the evening when Ian collapsed. Once you're inside of a great working like that, you can't stop. If you do, the spell will keep going and can go wild, dragging your magic with it. Thank the gods my sister was there. Viola has a talent for melding with another mage. She...supported him. Gave him some of her strength. He recovered, and she helped him complete the spell."

Mal's arms squeezed her tight. "But part of her magic, part of herself, was permanently left within Ian."

Now that she had twined herself with Malcolm, she understood for the first time how deeply intimate it was. To be forever connected to a man she did not love, a part of herself lost inside of him? That would be horrible.

"Great Mother," she whispered, and Mal released her. Did he think her disgusted with him? She put a hand on his chest, and let her affection for him flood through their magical connection.

He finished the story. "It took them most of the last two years to come to terms with it, and I'm not certain that either has relinquished hope that they might one day reverse what happened. But Viola is strong, and Ian is a good man. They married once the families found out they were pregnant."

"Oh! No one has ever said Viola's husband's name to me. I didn't realize you were talking about the same person. Although, if it feels to her and Ian the way this feels for us, I can understand why they slept together."

"I didn't ask about that part. I am her brother, and there are some things I don't wish to know about my sisters."

Etta chuckled. It was an awful tale, but perhaps something good had come of it. If Viola and Ian had found each other, had made something out of the tragedy, that was worth celebrating.

"How does your mother come into the story?"

Mal frowned. "After what happened, she forbade me to take another apprentice. But I was already a step ahead of her. I swore I would never do magic again." He traced an idle finger around one of the symbols on the stone, a representation of fire. "I fled society, and bought my estate. I never thought to be back in London during the season again, much less to find you there, in need of training."

"And your sister? Was she also forbidden to teach magic?"

This time, Mal traced the symbol for water, and shook his head. "With part of her magic tied to Ian, she has to be careful. Her gift is stronger than his, but the part of it in him is only available to her when they're together. And even then, it has become almost as much his magic as hers. Sometimes the things that once came easily to her overwhelm them both. So it isn't so much that she's forbidden to teach, as that she is still relearning her own limits." He rubbed her upper arm and gathered her close, wrapping both of his arms around her. "We'll talk Mother around. You need to convince her you'll act in the best interests of the clan."

"I would never hurt any of you, I promise." She spoke the words against his chest. It was a lovely chest, firm and rounded, probably by work on his estate. If he had eschewed magic, he'd have to do everything by hand.

When he'd stated his vow not to do magic in harsh, grating tones, she'd ached for him. Her magic defined her—even without being used—in ways she could never imagine renouncing. But he had, and now that meant he could not help her. Neither could Viola, for very different reasons. Lady Hazelby still held all of her hopes.

Dallying with Mal was folly. Not only because his mother would disapprove, but because her fears had been proven.

Yet she did not pull away from him now. When they'd come together, she'd lost herself. She'd given in to the passion, embracing it with a fervor that had split her open, leaving her vulnerable. And Mal had admitted that he could not—no, would not—do magic anymore. He might desire her as a woman, but she was also a witch. How long could she live with someone who denied his own magic?

8

---

1 January 1888

*It's Hogmanay, and we have had an appropriately dark-haired
stranger as our first-foot. He came from the Tennessee side of the
Roan, in need of a midwife. I took Etta with me, and we assisted in
the birth of a beautiful baby girl, who had decided she wanted to
enter the world foot-first in deference to the holiday. I'm glad the
boy came for me. He and his wife are far too young, only sixteen
and fifteen respectively, but he showed his maturity today. Either
the mother or the child—or both—would have died if I hadn't
been there.*

*When we arrived back at the cabin, I sent Etta out to do the chores
and told Fayt I wanted another child. I'm only thirty-two. It isn't
too late to try again. From his response, he agrees.*

-from the journal of Aileana Fay Cook

Malcolm climbed out of the carriage and turned to help his mother out. Theirs was the first vehicle to arrive because they had chosen not to stop for luncheon at the turn-off as the others had.

He stayed where he was as Mother moved toward the house. Two of his teenaged cousins, Seonag and Ainsley, hopped down with only a token pressure on his hand. They were squabbling about something again, but in a good-natured way, and they quickly surpassed his mother and went into the house.

Etta appeared at the carriage door and he lifted his arm once more. She took it, but didn't meet his gaze. He'd had his tongue between her legs last night, had lapped at her sensitive flesh until her body shook with pleasure, and he wanted more than anything to pull her into his arms now. But she'd been perfectly circumspect in the carriage and was even now trying to pretend that the hand holding her arm was not attached to a man whose cock had been inside her mouth only hours before.

He was under no particular obligation not to stare at that mouth and picture her lips parting over him again. He hadn't been able to see well last night since she'd been shadowed from the stone's glow by his body, but he remembered every exquisite sensation. Her warm wetness enveloping him, her tongue dragging along his length...

He tore his gaze from her lips and turned his attention back to the house. Viola was sensitive to auras and his was going to be nearly molten with desire. That was not something he wanted his sister to see, even if he could disguise the bulge in his trousers from more mundane eyes.

Etta pulled away from his grasp and followed his mother and cousins up the crushed stone path to the massive front doors of the family estate. Viola wasn't there to greet them, but as they approached, Ian stepped out onto the drive.

Ian had his own property to the west, and he'd brought Viola here for her confinement because it was more convenient to the town and the local midwife. Now that the family had arrived, the need for the midwife was less acute, but the fact that it was a Fay property meant it was still the best place for Viola to give birth. Mal appreciated that his brother-in-law truly cared about the welfare of his sister.

Considering their situation, he'd been afraid that Ian would have no affection for her at all. It was why he'd gone to their wedding, to try and give Viola a way out. Instead, it appeared that their unusual connection had blossomed into affection. Perhaps love. But that didn't make his role in their situation any less appalling, or relieve his guilt.

"Welcome, Lady Hazelby, Lord Malcolm," Ian said. "Viola is resting, but she'll be down for tea. The girls have already gone off to claim a bedchamber." His voice had a pleasant burr, one he nearly lost when in London, but which returned almost instantly once he crossed the border. Mal's fingers tapped against his leg. He didn't know how to talk to Ian now, or how to bridge the chasm he'd created when he pushed his friend to summon power he couldn't control. He settled for as much of a smile as he could muster and a nod to acknowledge the welcome.

Ian turned to Etta, his handsome face relaxed, a warm smile on his lips.

Mother, as the highest ranking, ought to have introduced Ian to her, but she did not. The silence stretched a moment too long, and Mal wasn't sure if his mother meant to snub Etta, or Ian. He stepped to Etta's side. To hell with formality.

"Ian, this is Miss Etta Mae Cook from North Carolina. Etta, may I present my brother-in-law, Lord Ian MacAlasdair, Baron Dromoss."

Ian held his hand out to Etta, who grasped it and shook. Ian looked a little taken-aback by this gesture, but then Etta remembered herself and curtseyed over his hand.

"It's a pleasure to meet you, Miss Cook."

"As it is to meet you, Lord Dromoss."

"Won't you come inside? One of the maids will take you to your room so you can rest until your own maid arrives with the rest of your things. We aren't formal here, but it amuses Viola to dress for tea."

"Thank you. That would be lovely." She allowed him to draw her hand onto his arm, and he led her into the house. Inside, he passed her off to a maid, and the two women disappeared into one of the wings, a footman following behind with Etta's valise.

"I was surprised to get your telegram about Miss Cook," Ian said. "Is she truly a Fay?"

"So she says." Mother handed her coat to another waiting maid. "I will go see Viola."

Ian's expression said that he wanted to protest, but could not think of a good way to do it without offending his mother-in-law. More to the point, without offending the mother-in-law who had never accepted that her eldest daughter had married a lowly baron. And most especially not that she had done so only *after* conceiving said baron's child.

Malcolm knew she had higher hopes for Olivia, his youngest sister, but doubted Olivia had similar aspirations. Olivia wanted to travel and write books. Marriage to a titled gentleman was not one of her prized dreams.

His mother started up the grand stair, leaving Mal and Ian alone.

"Etta is a Fay," Mal said once his mother was out of earshot. "Distant from our branch of the family, but a Fay. She's descended from Marianne."

"The one who eloped with the Irishman?"

"Aye, that's the one." Falling back into their old conversational habits came more easily than he'd expected. He should have sought out Ian sooner. "Etta is her great-great-granddaughter, descended entirely through the maternal line."

"She has a powerful talent. I should have guessed it. You lot lost some potency with all of those lads as ancestors."

Mal ignored the playful dig at his antecedents, and focused on the important bit. "Her powerful talent is the reason she's here. Her mother died a few months ago and the States haven't lifted the ban on Southern magic use since their civil war. With magic waning in popularity here, she needs a teacher."

"You're not thinking of asking Viola?" Ian stiffened.

Mal understood why, and could have punched himself. "Of course not."

The frown didn't leave Ian's face, though he relaxed a trifle. "Good. Things are still…not right with her magic. And pregnancy and magic don't mix well under the best of circumstances."

"Mother and Muireall are dragging their heels, but no one is going to ask Viola to be her teacher. Etta knows that."

"Why not you and Lady Hazelby?"

"Do you think that's wise? You, of all people?"

Ian shrugged, as though the greatest mistake of Malcolm's life were a minor concern. "With your mother overseeing the training, things won't have a chance to go as wrong as they did with us."

"Mother isn't going to want me anywhere near Etta and her magic."

Ian scoffed. "Why not?"

"Because she isn't blind. She's already seen that I'm interested in Etta."

Now it wasn't so much a scoff as a guffaw. "Truly? You've never been a rake, but you've not looked twice at an eligible woman in all of our years of carousing together. You'd marry an American lass?"

"I'd marry Etta. Her being American isn't part of my thought process."

"Isn't it, indeed? Her world is not yours, brother."

Mal winced. Ian might or might not mean the fraternal reminder as a gibe, but it felt like one.

"It is now. She's here, and she'll stay."

"There are other mages out there in the world who could teach her."

"Those mages aren't Fay. She's family, and we'll stick by her. Mother won't like it, but I'm not going to give her a choice."

~

VIOLA DID NOT APPEAR FOR TEA, OR FOR BREAKFAST THE NEXT morning, which worried Mal enough that he went upstairs near noon to see her. She was asleep when he entered her room, propped on a sofa with her head lolling to the side and her feet elevated. An open book rested on her swollen belly, the pages fanned out.

He crossed the room to take the book away. Almost without thought, his magic sought hers. Where once their gifts had merged seamlessly—her spring water and rain instinctively fitting to his citrus and light—now a jagged piece stuck out, rubbing and poking. She woke.

"Mal," she murmured. Her voice was soft, and cracked a little with sleep. He knelt beside the sofa and stroked her hair back from her face, withdrawing his magic at the same time. He hoped she hadn't noticed.

"Hello, love." She was so beautiful, his little sister. Almost a perfect copy of their mother, except she had their father's bright blue eyes. A fresh wave of shame rushed through him. How could he have endangered her?

"What time is it?" Her practical question brought him back from the past.

"Almost noon."

"Oh, dear." She made a face and shifted. Something audibly popped, and she winced. Then she caught his horrified expression, and prodded him on the shoulder. "Don't worry, that's normal." She arched her back and groaned. "But I've missed breakfast. I meant to come down. I can't seem to stay awake for more than an hour or so, and then I can't stay asleep for more than two. Is Mother cross?"

"Only a little. She's had to hold up conversation with the whole clan for two whole meals now, when what she wanted to do was ignore Etta."

"Ah, this mysterious cousin of ours. I had planned to see her in the drawing room before dinner last night, but I fell asleep. I had a burst of energy in the middle of the pregnancy, but now I can't escape this lethargy." She kicked one foot into the air, and then put it back on its pillow. "And my ankles swell terribly if I stand too long. So I sit here, and take a turn about the house a few times a day."

Mal shifted to her feet and rubbed one of her ankles. "Are you hungry?"

Her head dropped back against the cushions and she sighed. "Yes, but I won't eat much. Cook knows what to send. The babes' favorite activity is shoving wee limbs into Mum's digestive organs, so I eat small amounts throughout the day."

"Would you like me to bring Etta up after you eat?" He switched to the other ankle.

"No, but I do want to meet her." She poked him with her toe. "Your aura keeps going all red when you think about her."

Mal dropped her foot and she grunted but then laughed,

her belly jiggling with mirth. "Och, goddess, your face." She chortled, and poked him again.

He glowered at her. "I suppose it's useless to try and keep secrets."

"Always has been. Why should it be any different now?" Her smile was bland, but her blue eyes were as merry as a faire-day sky.

"I think I'm in love with her."

The smile opened to an O of surprise, and Viola pushed back against her cushions. "It's time for one of my walks, so I'll eat and then find you in the music room. I need to meet this girl." She tried to sit up, and Malcolm jumped to help her.

"Och, I feel as ungainly as a selkie on the beach before it sheds its sealskin."

"You're using Ian's brogue."

"Survival technique. Besides, it feels natural to me now."

Now meant 'after part of myself got stuck inside of him.' But they'd become accustomed to avoiding specific mention of what happened, so Mal didn't ask again.

"I'll ring for your maid, and go find Etta."

She stretched, arms over her head, and then relaxed, resting her hands on her belly. "I'll be a half hour at least."

"We'll be there." He kissed her forehead. "I love you."

"I love you too." She smiled at him as he pulled the cord that would ring in the servant's hall, summoning Viola's maid. "Off with you now. Dorcas will insist on dressing me, even though I've explained that putting on anything resembling a fashionable gown only makes me feel like a sow."

"Selkie is more accurate. You're lovelier than ever, dearest sister. Swollen ankles and all." He grinned as she made a shooing motion and growled at him.

"Get out of here before I manage to waddle over and box your ears."

He was halfway out the door when she called, "I'm very glad Mother made you come, Malcolm." He halted, arrested, on the threshold. "My babies need all of the family together, and I need you. There are dark times coming."

Mal looked over his shoulder at Viola. She stood beside her dressing table, both hands holding her belly as though she needed to protect the two precious lives within. And perhaps she did. He hadn't wanted to be here, but she was right. His mother was right. The twins needed him, and he would join the spell that welcomed them to the world.

"I'm glad I came, too," he said, and closed the door.

He found Etta outside under the patchy sunlight, as he'd known he would. She did not like being indoors. He suspected that the grand houses of his family intimidated her, and she didn't like the feeling. She'd told him about her mother's cabin in the woods, and he imagined that she'd give almost anything to be back there now. It sounded like a hard life, but it was the life she knew and understood.

She straightened from an examination of a herb and smiled at him.

He took her hand and squeezed it. "My sister apologizes for missing the last few meals. She wants to meet you, though, so she's going to eat something in her suite, then meet us in the music room in a little while." He put her hand on his arm, and they walked out farther into the gardens.

"Is she feeling well? I don't need to meet her yet if she wants to rest."

"Well enough for being so near her delivery. She said it's time for some exercise anyway."

Etta watched him with concern in her expression. "My magical talents don't run toward healing, but I've assisted my mother with many pregnant women over the years. I'd be happy to help, if she likes."

"You can ask her. But my mother's talents do run toward healing, so I'm guessing she already did some complex diagnostic spellwork yesterday afternoon when we arrived."

"Oh. That would explain the surge of magic I felt while Beth helped me change from my travel dress. But with so many mages running around, I didn't wonder much more about it."

"Yes, that was her. No one else has cause to be casting anything that powerful at the moment. And Ian says Viola hasn't done much since she got pregnant. Apparently the hormonal imbalances cause control issues."

"Something to keep in mind, should I someday choose to have children." This time, she didn't look at him, but kept her gaze trained on the path through the kitchen vegetables. Mal steered them away, into the greenhouse. The walls were frosted glass, and there was enough foliage to shield them from view.

Once inside, he glanced around to make sure they were alone, and then pulled Etta into his arms. "Don't tease me." He braced his magic so it would not make the leap into her, and kissed her.

Her lips parted, and her tongue slipped into his mouth. He met its thrust with a stroke of his own, and slid a hand down her back. She wore a regular morning dress, and the damned thing had a bustle, so he couldn't feel her lovely round are as he had yesterday. He gripped what he could and yanked her against him. The skirt had little structure in front save a few layers of fabric, and his erection prodded her lower belly.

Etta moaned into his mouth and rubbed her body along his. He abandoned her lips and pressed kisses onto her neck, then down. The bustle was unfortunate, but the neckline was perfect, scooped low enough to reveal the tops of her breasts. He traced her collarbone with his tongue, then lower, over the mounds and into the cleft between.

It wasn't enough. He guided her to a stone bench and they sat together. He wrapped one arm around her, and with the other he nudged at the top of the bodice. She arched her back as he pulled. One perfect breast popped out, now propped up by the stiff fabric underneath, its taut brown tip pointed upward as though seeking him. He groaned and took the nipple into his mouth, suckling it, and then dragged his tongue back and forth across it until she gasped and moaned.

"I want you so badly." Her magic caressed the edges of his, and he almost let go—almost allowed their gifts to mesh as they had last night. But now was not the time.

He released her nipple, loving the way it glistened, wet from his mouth. "I want you, too."

She tangled her hands in his hair. "Even if your parents would cast you out for being with me?"

"They won't." At least Father wouldn't. He'd all but given his blessing to the match before they left for Scotland. Mother...Mother would have to get used to the idea, that was all.

Mal swirled a fingertip around her slick areola. She pushed into his touch, and a heady lightness filled his chest. He'd never had a lover like her. He'd only ever bedded willing women, but they'd all sought his pleasure, not their own. He liked to please them, but he was always aware that he did it because he wanted to, not because his lover expected him to.

Etta demanded pleasure and gave it in equal measure. Even now, she'd managed to slip her hand into his lap. Her fingers stroked over him as he played with her, and she tilted her head up to kiss him again.

Hinges creaked as the greenhouse door opened. Etta

pulled away and tugged her bodice back in place. But she wasn't embarrassed, only circumspect, because she smiled and nuzzled him with her nose. Then she stood, and walked over to an orange tree. She touched one of the tiny unripened fruits, and smiled at the gardener who walked by with a canvas bag full of soil. On his heels came two of the teenaged cousins, each holding potted plants and pestering the beleaguered man with questions. They must be studying agrimancy at school, and wanted to get ahead.

Mal remained seated, due to the obvious swelling in his trousers. Once his erection subsided, he went to her and they left the greenhouse.

ON THE WAY BACK INSIDE, THEY WERE WAYLAID BY NEW arrivals. The rest of the far-flung Fay clan had descended on the house in preparation for Viola's labor. Etta shrank a little into his side, at first, and he was reminded that she'd grown up nearly alone, with the nearest family a fifteen-minute walk away over a mountain ridge, and the closest town a two-hour walk. She hadn't socialized much, and then it had been in small groups. Clan Fay was large, loud, and very Scottish, despite the French name.

Some of the non-magical members of the family hadn't come, and some who had come were magical, but were related by marriage, not blood. Mal said people's names and approximate relationship to her as they passed, but without much hope that she'd remember any of it later.

They kept to the outskirts of the entrance hall, which resembled the platform at a train station, and managed to avoid being entangled in any conversations until they were almost on the stairs.

A very petite woman stepped out from the group near the

steps, and said, "Hello, Mal." Sorcha Fay was the shortest member of the family. Her blonde hair, so pale that the family white streak barely showed at her left temple, only brushed the top of his chest as she hugged him. But what she lacked in height, she made up for in curves and lush beauty, with a heart-shaped face and starlight-pale skin.

"Hello, Sorcha."

She released him, and contemplated Etta.

Etta gaped back, nearly vibrating with curiosity. He couldn't blame her. Of all his extended family, the Seeress of Skye was the most elusive. Sorcha spent most of her time in the ancestral Fay lands, and rarely left the Hebrides. Being in her presence was like being near a magical power center, almost akin to making the yearly pilgrimage to drink from the fairy spring on the property and then go swimming, nude, in the sea. As children, he and Viola had called it the salt-and-sweet trip, since they invariably swallowed both kinds of water in quantity.

"Etta, this is our cousin Sorcha Fay. Sorcha, this is Etta Mae Cook, our cousin from America."

"I ken who you are," Sorcha said in the musical tones of the Scottish Isles. "I Saw you." She hadn't shifted her gaze from Etta, and she wore an enigmatic expression.

"Oh," Etta said. "Did you have a vision, then?"

"I did." Sorcha still stared at Etta as though she could see deep into her soul. Then she grinned. "But we'll have time to speak of it later. Go and see Viola. She could use a sister to talk to, after what her husband has put her through this last month."

Mal wasn't sure what she meant by that, but it warmed him to hear Sorcha so casually refer to Etta as Viola's sister. As though their relationship were already established. And, if Sorcha had seen it, he had even more reason to hope.

9

---

22 February 1888

He is gone. Oh, Great Spirit, how can my Fayt be gone?
Etta weeps.
I have cried my heart empty.

-from the journal of Aileana Fay Cook

In the music room, Viola sat at the pianoforte. Her fingers danced on the keys, producing a mournful melody unlike anything Etta had ever heard.

Her childhood had been full of song, but it was the sound of fiddles and homemade drums, of reed flutes and penny-whistles. There'd been talk of raising money for an organ at the county building in Bakersville, but times were tough, and the talk always faded. Even at the musicale in Raleigh, she'd not seen anyone playing a pianoforte.

Each separate depression on the keyboard connected to a piece of Etta's soul, making her resonate in echo to whatever melodic alchemy was hidden beneath the lid.

She stepped toward the instrument, each footfall meeting a note, like a spelled automaton. Her hand reached out, and her fingers rested on the great expanse of wood that both created and amplified the sound.

Etta's eyes closed and for the rest of the song she simply experienced the world as music.

After it ended, she opened her eyes again to see Viola watching her with a bemused expression.

"Did you like it?"

"Very much. I saw this instrument in the house in London, but I did not hear anyone play it. It's lovely."

"Thank you. Mal is better than me, but he rarely plays anymore."

Etta frowned at Mal's sister. Her features were like her mother's, with the same pale skin and arching dark brows, but there was a resemblance to Mal, too. Viola's nose was a little smaller, more pert and feminine, but she had the same piercing blue eyes and a similar wide mouth, only with a bowed upper lip like her mother's rather than the smoother line of Malcolm's.

She also had a defined streak of silver, arching above her left eye and disappearing into a soft bun at the nape of her neck. The Fay streak. Etta's fingers twitched to touch the place where she had only a strand or two coming in.

"Don't pay any attention to my deluded sister." Malcolm sat beside Viola on the bench and put his arm around her. The familiarity and affection was almost shocking, after the cold distance she'd witnessed between all of the other members of the Seward family, even Malcolm and his older brother Giles.

Viola put her head on her brother's shoulder and smiled at Etta. "So, Ian tells me that you're here to be trained. Are you a glutton for punishment, or has someone told you lies about the family teaching methods?"

The warmth and humor in Viola's words, and her absolute lack of formality, eased Etta's anxiety about meeting Mal's sister. She'd feared to meet another Lady Hazelby, especially with such a pronounced physical resemblance. But Viola was far more like her brother than her mother in personality.

The friendly question prompted an honest answer. "It is the simplest solution to my problem. I cannot learn in America, and none of the schools here in Britain still teach Lilias's Way."

"I know. It's a pity," Viola said. "This insistence on idleness and frivolity is destroying more than the upper classes. Just because Lilias did actual, practical things with magic, anyone who casts a useful spell is suddenly considered a tradesman. As if that were something to be ashamed of, anyway!"

Mal laughed. "Viola is a bit of a rebel. She had to be withdrawn from her finishing school because she incited the other girls to riot."

"Did you?" Etta grinned. "What were you protesting?"

"Oh, a number of things." She rubbed her belly absently. "Teenage girls are already prone to believing that the rest of the world is out to get them. I only had to show them some examples of how that was actually true before we all decided to rise up."

"Olivia was so disappointed that she hadn't been sent to school yet," Mal said. "And Father decided after that to have the girls tutored at home."

Etta laughed.

The door swung open, and the laugh turned into a choked cough. Lady Hazelby strode into the music room. "It is time for you to be tested."

Etta stumbled forward, finally breaking contact with the pianoforte. Mal helped Viola to her feet.

"Do you need my assistance, Mother?" Viola asked.

"No. You should rest. With the rest of the clan's arrival, there will be so much magic suffusing the house that it will keep you from true sleep until the babies come."

Viola crossed to Etta and took her hands. The touch was gentle, her magic cool and strong. Etta had the impression of depth and power, reminiscent of the North Atlantic Drift. But unlike Muireall's sea-salt and brine, Viola's magic tasted like spring water and rain, sweet and pure. The energy swirled sun-wise, gathering strength for the coming birth.

A little of that energy passed into Etta, who squeezed tight and wished Viola could be her teacher. But she was committed to this path, and she would not falter because of fear.

The two women stepped back, and their clasped hands parted. Mal stirred in Etta's direction, but she glared at him. Instead, he stared at her, his expression full of affection and hope.

Etta followed Lady Hazelby out and into the hall. They walked down the wide passage, through a drawing room and outside, into the kaleyard. It was a working garden, growing vegetables and herbs in full summer leaf.

Would they halt there, in the garden, to do some kind of earth-based magic? They didn't. Lady Hazelby led her down a gravel path into the larger, formal gardens, and then out again, through a hedge and along a stone wall, to a stream.

They walked along the bank of the stream for a long time, until it widened and flattened out at a rocky ford. There, they crossed. Muireall waited on the other side, and together, the three of them started up the far hill.

The climb made Etta homesick, and a little angry that she hadn't been warned where they were going. She hadn't had a good hike in months, and now she was forced to do it in a dress, with less-than-appropriate footwear. She wasn't wearing decorative slippers as she had with her ballgown, but these heeled boots were meant for city walking, not a muddy hike to the top of a Scottish mountain.

Yet Lady Hazelby and Muireall wore similar garments, and both women fairly glided over the path. If they could do it, so could Etta.

Lady Hazelby halted and turned, looking out over the estate of Emberlach. Etta stared at the rolling expanse, noting crofter's cottages, grazing beasts and fields of potatoes, and the road that led to the village. The town itself, and the loch fed by the streams, was hidden behind the bulk of the next peak.

"To truly test you," Le Fay said, "we will have to take you to Skye, where Lilias was born. But we are near, and the loch beside the village joins with another, and another still, until they empty out into the sea. It is enough."

Etta grasped fabric from either side of her skirt and held it tight.

"To begin," Lady Hazelby said, "you must continue on the path, to the summit. There, you will find a cairn. Choose a stone from the cairn, and bring it back to me."

"Is there a criteria for choosing a stone? Randomly? Will one call to me?"

Neither woman answered.

Etta pressed her lips together and continued her hike.

Compared to her mountains, these were barren and forlorn. She missed the scent of evergreen sap and decaying leaves, although the mist that hung in the air was reminiscent of the Great Smokies.

At the peak, she found the cairn. Its stones were a mixture of jagged and smooth, and Etta had no idea how she was supposed to choose one to take.

The very idea felt wrong. Weren't people supposed to add stones to cairns? She was sure that she'd heard that somewhere. Cairns could be raised for many reasons, and passersby added to them over the years, replacing stones as weather wore them away, until the purpose of the rock was long forgotten, except perhaps by the earth beneath.

Etta circled the cairn, studying its shape, letting her gaze drift over the stones, hoping one would speak to her. Her boot knocked against a loose stone in the path, and she picked it up. The edges had long since worn smooth, and she ran her thumb over the cream-and-brown surface, feeling the irregularities made by veins of different substances and tiny crystalline flecks. The stone warmed in her palm.

She walked over and placed it on the cairn.

Her inner landscape, her sense of the physical and magical planes, shifted. Belatedly, she remembered to open her Sight.

The cairn was not simply a conglomeration of rocks. It was a magical nexus. By feeding it with her stone, she'd raised the deep power to the surface.

She reached inside, not with her hands, but with her mind and her magic. The nexus was not obscenely powerful. It was nothing like as strong as the North Atlantic Drift, or even the little nexus formed by the confluence of two small creeks into a larger river where she and her mother had often gone to meditate. But it held within itself a stillness, a certainty of belonging, and it made Etta ache for what she'd lost and left behind.

She sought that center, and it stretched back to surround her. For the space of eternity, hung suspended between heartbeats, Etta existed as a being of stone. She became adamant, her skin giving way grudgingly and slowly to wind and rain. Her bones were the mountain, and her soul burned with its secret fire.

There, in the heart of the earth-nexus, she found what Lady Hazelby had asked her to retrieve. A stone, yes, but no pebble. This was a spirit gem, a thing that existed on a different plane from the physical, but which could be brought through with some effort. Etta had read of such things, but never encountered one herself. Did something like this lie at the heart of every nexus?

And, more importantly, did she have the skill and the strength to wrench it free?

Her mind's hand grasped the spirit gem, and her entire being resonated with its power. It was the embodiment of stasis, of endurance, and did not budge. How could she fight a mountain?

She would have to be like the wind and the rain, coaxing and dancing across its surface, gentle but inexorable, working into a tiny fissure until the fissure became a crack, and the crack cleaved the gem from the cairn.

In the early days of her training, Ma had tried her best to show Etta simple spells. They were things that Ma's Gran had taught her, but that she could never make work, because her magic didn't follow the same rules as Marianne's. Etta's magic had, and one of those basic elemental alliance spells had been used to predict the weather.

She sketched out the anchor lines of the spell net, forming the symbols for water, earth, and air. But instead of weaving the spell she remembered, she sank the anchors into the nexus.

The leyline began to draw magic out of her, pulling through her net. Etta clutched at the spell, trying to keep control, drawing power from everywhere she could grasp, and suddenly Mal was with her. His magic snapped into her, aligning again as it had that day by the stream. It gave her the balance she needed to wrest her net back and invert it.

Once the symbols faced the correct direction, the energy reversed its flow, and what she'd hoped would happen did—

the spirit stone trembled, as though rocked by a strong wind, then flowed out to her as though carried on a creek.

She grabbed the stone, and came back to a sense of her body with a shudder. Only then did she hear Mal's voice in her head. He was frantic, almost screaming.

Not again. Not again!

He said it over and over, and when she connected with him to tell him it was all right—to tell him she was sorry—he ripped his magic away from hers. She gasped, the pain tearing through her like a scythe. Her fingers closed convulsively around a cool, hard weight in her right hand and some of the ache receded.

In her palm, in place of the little rock she'd offered, was a chunk of what appeared to be tourmaline, all purples and greens and reds and browns. She closed her fingers around the spirit gem, and looked out to the west. The cloud cover had broken enough for her to see the sun, swollen and red, on the horizon. The day was almost done.

She went back to Le Fay and Lady Hazelby.

The marchioness accepted the cairn's stone with no expression. She did not praise Etta's work, or critique her methods. She said nothing. Instead, she walked away, back down the slope toward the house.

Etta followed, and worried. Had she passed, by retrieving the stone, or had her inadvertent link with Malcolm caused her to fail?

10

18 May 1888

*I have not had the heart to write for many months, but Etta has
had her first woman's blood, and though I do not wish for the
reminder, it has forced to me acknowledge that I did not die with
my husband. Life continues. Magic swells and blooms inside of her.
I wish Gran were here. Etta's magic feels so much like hers, and so
little like mine. I will do my best, but I fear she will learn little from
me. Is it time to send her to my kin across the water?*

Forgive me, Etta, but I cannot. I cannot lose you, too.

-from the journal of Aileana Fay Cook

Mal paced in his father's study. He'd acted the
pleasant host for the Fay relations who'd
arrived after Muireall and Mother left, and now
he needed to not have to look at another human for a few
minutes. He couldn't ignore the magic surging about, but he

could close himself in a dark room and shut the door. With the marquess still in London and Ian not leaving Viola's side, this was the quietest place in the house.

What was Mother making Etta do? Would it be anything like the tests he and Viola had been subject to over the years, or would she devise something diabolical and new?

His mother wouldn't deliberately sabotage Etta's chances, but there was no denying that she held a great deal of animosity toward their American relation. Did she feel threatened? Was it the prospect of losing Mal? Of being supplanted in her position with the Fay clan? Because, once she was trained, Etta would be a formidable witch. Strong enough to become the next Le Fay, if that was what she wanted.

Muireall hadn't seemed particularly threatened. She worried more for the school than for herself. But Etta had power, and a direct matrilineal descent from Lilias. If she chose to try and lead the clan, many of the members would follow her. The rest of the family traced their Fay lineage through a male: his own grandfather, Silas, Earl of Clary, and Muireall's father Robert, Baron Darrow. Patrilineal descent was inherently weaker, and more likely to result in non-magic offspring.

Etta was a daughter of a daughter of a daughter. And those women had married gifted men. Her father was the son of a Cherokee shaman and a French Chanteur missionary, a sect that worshiped magical gifts as proof of the divine on earth. Her maternal grandfather was a mountain mage of mixed Scottish and Choctaw descent. When Etta finished her training, the Fay family would be in for some interesting changes.

Something tugged at his magic, and he gasped. Then the tug became a pull, and he fell out of the chair to the floor. He tried to erect barriers, but it was too late. When he opened his eyes again, he did not see the study, but a cairn, and Etta's hands grasping at a half-formed spell net.

His body stiffened even as his magic instinctively rose to help her. They meshed more deeply than they had when he'd had his mouth on her, so completely that when she flicked her fingers, his own twitched in response.

No. Not again. He couldn't do this again, could not cast another spell. How many times had he tried, in the days following the accident, only to have his workings fall apart? His confidence had shattered, and after one bad spell he'd almost destroyed his lodgings. So he'd sworn it—never again. He would never cast a spell again.

Not again. Never again. Not again!

The mantra repeated, over and over, and he curled into a ball on the floor of the study. He rocked and tried not to see Etta's hands, twisting threads of magic. He denied the sensation of power shifting and moving, and his hands making the shapes with hers. He screamed at her —*NOT AGAIN!*

But she didn't hear, and she didn't stop, and the spell coalesced. Then it was done.

She finally felt him, and tried to say something, but he didn't care. The spell was done. It was all he could contemplate, all he could see. The spell was done, and he needed to be free. He ripped his magic away from her, barely feeling the tearing pain that split through his skull.

He collapsed back onto the floor, panting. It was over. He was free.

He lay there on his side for what felt like a thousand years, still curled a little inward, eyes firmly shut, dragging deep lungfuls of air in and shoving them back out again in an attempt to calm his racing heart. The floorboards smelled of beeswax polish and lemon, and the simple scents finally brought him back to himself.

When everything had steadied—minutes or hours later, he couldn't tell—he dared to open his eyes.

The room swam in and out of focus, his Sight still open even though he hadn't willed it. The magic in the house nearly pulsed, and his gorge rose. He closed his Sight and swallowed the acid, but the deep thrum of an imminent spell remained. Oh, gods. It was time.

He sat up, wobbling as another wave of nausea and dizziness chased over him.

A knock sounded on the door, and Mal groaned. "What is it?"

The door swung in to reveal Kincaid, Ian's valet. "It's starting," he said. He lifted an eyebrow at Mal, seated on the floor, and then strode away down the hall.

Mal swore and pushed to his feet. He stumbled and caught himself on the cane-backed visitor's chair. It took another minute of deep, regular breathing to regain his balance. Then he walked carefully out into the hall, toward the central stair.

His mother was going to be angry she'd been gone when the labor pains began.

But when he moved from the side hall into the foyer, his mother was already gliding upstairs with Muireall, Etta in tow. He must have taken longer recovering than he'd realized. Mal hurried to catch them and fell into step beside Etta.

"What the hell happened?" he asked, low, so that no one else could hear.

Etta whispered back, her expression stricken. "I don't know. I'm so sorry, Mal. I didn't try to pull you in like that." She'd probably been hurt by his abrupt withdrawal, but he couldn't help that.

He deliberately relaxed his stiff muscles, seeking a calm place inside where he could regain some sanity. He was going to need it for what came next.

"You're going to have to practice seeking energy sources for your spells. My guess is that you never got beyond internal magic before."

She nodded. "Ma and I sometimes did what she called 'basking.' We would sit out in the sun, or lay in the creek—that sort of thing—absorbing power. But I never needed to draw from an outside source when I cast a spell, no."

"I didn't realize that, or I wouldn't have shown you how to merge. When you needed power, your magic instinctively went for a source that it knew. Me."

"I don't know how to apologize, Mal. I would never—"

"I know. We'll discuss it more later. For now, do you think you passed?"

"I haven't a clue. Your mother hasn't said a word to me." Etta gestured at Lady Hazelby's receding skirts. "She and Muireall marched in here and went right up. I'm not even sure I'm supposed to be following them. Or if this is part of the test."

Mal took the gesturing hand into his. "You're supposed to follow them. We all are. They're going to Viola's room."

"Is something wrong?" Her fingers tightened. "Is it the babies?"

"Not wrong, but it is the twins. They're coming."

"Oh." She stopped, and he had to stop with her. "Are you sure I'm supposed to be there?"

"You're a Fay. You're supposed to be there. You'll see." He tugged her along.

At the top of the stairs, they turned toward the family wing. Viola's door stood open. Beyond, the room was filled by members of Clan Fay.

Etta halted in the hallway, and Mal stopped with her. She stared into the room, and he realized she was afraid. Afraid to be rejected? Afraid to be found wanting? He pulled her back a bit, so they couldn't be seen from the room, and then put his arms around her. She vibrated with tension, her arms shaking where they pressed against his sides.

He stroked a finger down her jaw. He wasn't entirely recovered, but he had been part of the blood-unity spell before. Many times. She needed his experience and reassurance now, more than his lingering anxiety. "Don't worry. This isn't another test. This will not be anything like that, although it will involve...connection. Births in our clan are always special occasions." He captured her mouth. She kissed him back, but with an edge of desperation.

Mal hugged her again, hard, and then grasped her hand. He had to pull her through the doorway. They stepped into chaos. By the fireplace, Sorcha, Muireall and Muireall's two brothers, Rob and Neill, held hands and chanted together, crafting the net for what would be the birthing spell. That was the source of the deep thrum and pulse downstairs. Over next to the window, Muireall's two daughters giggled over a book they held between them. The family's Book of Shadows and Light.

Uncle Robert, the patriarch of Muireall's part of the family, sat on the floor with his grandsons and baby granddaughter. Muireall's son Bruce, who was ten, looked like he would rather be anywhere than in a room with a woman about to give birth. Little Rabbie, Rob's son, was only five, and took his cues from his cousin. Wee Eilidh, Neill's lass, was nearly three. But they were Fay.

There were others in the room—descendents of Lilias's cousins and siblings—laughing and talking and casting minor spells to supplement the main one. Some of them had children balanced on hips or settled on laps, or playing at their sides.

The younger ones wouldn't be present the whole time, but they had to be here when the spell-net was completed.

They were all the members of the family with magic. There were two other wee ones who had no gifts, children of Robert and Neill, who were elsewhere in the house with their non-Fay mothers.

Viola leaned against one of her bedposts. She wore a loose nightgown and had her hair in a messy pile on her head. Ian stood behind her, rubbing her back in slow circles. He was the only person in the room not a Fay by blood. Normally, a non-Fay father would not be allowed into the birthing, but with Viola's magic inside of him, his presence here was crucial.

Mother—standing by a basin of hot water, her hands soapy—frowned when Etta and Mal entered. For a moment, he thought she would say something, perhaps even to order Etta away, but Muireall glanced up from her chanting and gestured with her chin, directing them to go to Viola.

Neither of them would be allowed to escape. Mal did as asked, towing Etta along.

The spell had more weight here, closer to his sister. Muireall and the others shaped it, but Viola and her babies were the focus. Even with his Sight closed, he could feel it like a warm blanket. Would he be comforted as it wrapped around him, or stifled and unable to breathe?

He pushed away those negative thoughts and focused on Viola.

Her eyes were full of pain, and, despite what had just happened with Etta, he couldn't stop himself from reaching out to his sister. His magic was still bruised, but they sank into each other the way they always had, and some of her pain bled over into him. They'd helped each other through their childhood illnesses and injuries this way. It was odd, as ever, to feel the jagged piece of her gift that was still missing, in Ian.

His brother-in-law had retreated a few paces away, and now stood staring at Viola as though his world were being ripped apart at the seams. Mal hesitated, and then lifted a hand to Ian. Viola hissed at him, but he ignored her. Ian grasped the offered fingers, and Mal drew him into the link.

Ian trembled, but accepted Viola's pain, and gave Mal a nod. He'd probably been begging Viola to let him do this already. She was too stubborn, sometimes. With the link now in place, Ian let go of Mal's hand and returned to his wife.

"I dinna want—" she said.

"I *do* want," Ian interrupted.

"Let us do this for you," Mal said. He stroked his sister's hair, then kissed her forehead. Her skin was clammy, but her eyes were already clearer. Then a contraction seized her.

All three of them froze. Even shared, the pain was intense and overwhelming. Mal's muscles tensed, fighting the squeezing pressure.

Etta stepped forward and took Viola's hands. "Relax," she said. "Breathe." She rubbed her thumbs against the base of Viola's palms, and down onto her wrists. Her voice, with its flat, American accent, was pitched low, now, soft and soothing. "Let the pain wash over you. You are a rock in the river. It wears at you, but then it passes by."

The contraction eased, and Viola clutched at Etta's hands. "Thank you."

Etta frowned at Mal and Ian. "If you're going to share her pain, you have to relax, too. Don't tense and fight it. It is much easier to manage if you allow it to flow through you." Both men agreed, although Mal wasn't sure he'd be able to do it, at least not without a few tries. He'd never experienced pain like that before.

Mother came around from the bed and contemplated the group. She didn't look as disapproving as usual, but she was not pleased to see Etta taking what she must consider to be her place with her daughter. "Viola, come sit on the bed," she ordered.

Viola went, and Ian helped her onto the mattress. Mal lifted her legs and swung them onto the coverlet. Mother sat at her daughter's feet and began to massage them. With his magic tuned to Viola's, he felt the way her energy pooled and swirled. Both the gentle pressure of their mother's hands and the tiny threads of magic on certain parts of the feet and ankles helped bring the chaotic mess back into balance.

And all around them, the blood-unity spell took on an almost audible thrum. It was still more feeling than sound, but it throbbed in the air and made his skin tingle. His mother tied her minor healing magic into the greater spell matrix, and the vibrations traveled down the link with Viola and into his core. His hands trembled, and he curled them into fists, but that wasn't enough to stop the shaking.

He forced his attention away from the bed and to Etta. She watched everything, her gaze darting from Mother, to Viola, to Muireall, and back again, her brows drawn together in thought. "What is it?" he asked her.

She started at his voice, and then shook her head before her gaze focused on him. "It's so familiar. My mother used to do that, to the mothers she brought through labor. She hadn't gotten around to teaching me the exact points of pressure yet. Or maybe she wouldn't ever have. I don't have the healing gift."

"Not everyone does." Then he gasped as another contraction seized Viola. But this one didn't seem as all-consuming as the first, less like a wildfire and more like a gas flame. The sensation was focused and intense, but with a purpose. Whatever his mother was doing was working.

Muireall came over to the bed, then, and all of the family

members crowded in. Everyone touched someone else, either by holding hands, or holding the children, until the whole clan was linked, with Mal and Cecily holding Viola's hands, and Ian kneeling behind her, his hands on her bare shoulders. In one voice, Muireall and Cecily chanted, and the spell-casting began.

11

---

14 September 1889

Every day, Etta's magic grows stronger. She deserves a better teacher than me. I thought of sending her north, of finding someone who would forge a birth certificate in Maryland or Ohio so she could go to one of the schools in Philadelphia or Boston. But I couldn't ask her to lie about so big a part of herself. And with my parents dead, there is no one out West I'd entrust to keep her safe in one of the schools in St. Louis or San Francisco.

I am a selfish creature. San Francisco is a few days travel by rail, and an entire continent away. I don't want her even that far, but I would take that over an ocean, and a few weeks on a steamship. What if she finds with the Fay clan what I could never give her? What if she never wants to come back?

-from the journal of Aileana Fay Cook

The spell-net settled over the group and Etta gasped. Her hand in Mal's tightened, and his gripped hers back. On her other side was one of his cousins, a teenaged girl who had an untrained gift almost as strong as Etta's. The girl squeezed. It was odd to receive reassurance from someone at least five years her junior.

She'd opened her Sight so that she could better examine what Lady Hazelby was doing to Viola with the massage, and hadn't bothered to close it when the clan gathered. Now, she saw each strand of the spell like golden threads, wrapping about each family member like a creeper vine, sending tiny tendrils to grasp at their magical cores.

The threads grasped them all, some thicker or thinner, depending on the person's strength and age, and met in the middle in a complex weaving, full of symbols that were both strange and intensely familiar.

Pulses of light ran along the threads of the weaving like beads of dew down a spider's web, glistening in the dawn. Except that these webs formed shapes and figures, and each junction glowed bright as a star, shining in a spell-constellation.

Etta had never seen spellwork so complex and yet structured and balanced, not at the Glasgow school, and certainly not at home. Her mother Aileana's wild spells looked more like a thicket of bramble than a fine tapestry.

With a burst of light and heat, the net settled onto Viola. They'd been connected before, but only in a physical sense. Now, every family member was linked to Viola, and to each other. The sensations of rightness, of completion and home, of community and belonging, were so intense that Etta wept.

Mal hadn't been lying to make her feel better. She was supposed to be here. Her blood resonated with theirs, and the joy of it hummed and sang under her skin.

Gradually, the family members released each other's hands and wandered away. The children were carried out. But the sense of connection remained. The twins would be born into this magic, would come into the world with the absolute knowledge that they were part of something bigger than a single self.

Ma could not have given her that connection. Etta's grandmother Caoimhe had been a skip, with no magical talent, and her great-grandmother, the runaway Marianne, had been killed in a train accident while Aileana was still pregnant. There had been no other Fay family in America to cast this spell over Etta when she was born.

Oh, Ma. What did we both lose, because you chose Papa, and because Great-Gran chose Great-Grand-da?

Eventually, only Cecily, Muireall, Mal, and Etta remained in the room with the expectant parents. The contractions came and went, and with each one the spell-net flared in intensity. Etta had attended many births as her mother's assistant, and the familiar sights and sounds of labor were bittersweet with memories. Mal retreated to the adjoining dressing room whenever his mother checked Viola's cervix, but otherwise was far more attentive than any sibling she'd ever seen. Ian was Viola's rock, but that was typical for mountain husbands. Often, their wives labored in isolated cabins, miles from any other homestead, and there was nowhere else to go, even if a midwife came.

Etta's thoughts danced to her beloved home, so far away now. The other side of the world. She pictured the steeply pitched roof, meant to slough off winter snow, and the two chimneys, one for the kitchen hearth, and the other for her mother's medicinal brews. She remembered her little sleeping alcove, curtained off near the kitchen hearth, and the sight of Ma, pounding herbs on her worktable or stirring something in the big copper kettle over an open fire. Papa had wanted to buy her a stove, had talked of little else the winter he was killed.

A sudden gasp brought Etta's thoughts back to the here-and-now. Viola was walking the room between Ian and Cecily, and fluid seeped out between her legs.

"Excellent," Cecily said. "Things should progress more quickly now."

Etta stared at the trio. When had she started thinking of Lady Hazelby as Cecily? Another contraction struck Viola, and another gush of amniotic fluid dripped down her legs. Muireall already had towels ready, but the birthing spell seemed to be spangled throughout Viola now, even sparkling within the little puddle that had formed on the floorboards.

The spell must have stripped away the entire silly pretense in her mind. Titles meant nothing in this room. Only love and connection had value here.

On the thought, Etta stood and helped Muireall clean the amniotic fluid. If she was a part of this family, then she would work with them, not simply observe.

HOURS PASSED. THEY ALL TOOK BRIEF BREAKS, AND ETTA changed into one of her old outfits from home, a worn but serviceable dress with no corset, that wouldn't be ruined by assisting in a delivery.

Etta walked the room with the laboring mother, and since Viola's hand was on her arm, it was simple to delve into the birthing spell and seek a connection. The spell-net was woven through Viola's belly and into her womb, where it cradled the two pulsing lives within. What would they be like, when they emerged into the world?

Etta gasped as Viola screamed.

"She's in transition," Cecily said, and took her daughter

over to the birthing stool by the fireplace. "Almost time to push, love."

Ian and Mal stationed themselves behind Viola and to either side, so she could grasp their arms while she pushed.

Cecily knelt in front of her daughter and did a quick check of her cervix, palpating Viola's belly with her other hand. "Yes, it's time. You can push with the next contraction."

Etta stood ready with a clean length of sheeting, prepared to take one of the babes and clean and wrap it, before giving it to Viola to nurse. Muireall stood on Cecily's other side with another sheet, ready to accept the other twin.

Viola pushed. She cried out in a long, resonant wail, and a few seconds later pushed again. And again. And again, until a little, smooshed head passed through the birth canal and out into the world. Cecily delivered the rest of the tiny body, and handed the babe to Muireall.

"It's a boy," the smiling Scotswoman proclaimed.

"Aye," Viola gasped. Then she pushed again. The placenta came out, and Cecily placed it into a little dish behind her, then clamped and cut the baby's cord.

Another ripple of a contraction washed over Viola's belly and she fairly keened as she bore down into the birthing stool. She looked exhausted and yet she fought, holding tight to her brother and her husband, until a second head breeched the birth canal and her son's twin took a deep gasp of warm air.

Cecily handed the squalling infant to Etta and turned back to deliver the final placenta.

"It's a girl." Etta could not stop staring at the babe, tiny and red-pink and perfect, her little face a bit squashed and swollen, covered in blood and streaks of a white waxy substance. After Cecily cut the second cord, Etta wiped the wee lass clean, and then handed her to her father.

Ian stared into his daughter's face and—despite a grin

that near split his cheeks—he wept. His tears dripped onto her forehead as he leaned to kiss her. "My lass, my love," he murmured.

Viola was already cradling the boy to her breast, and he suckled eagerly. She chuckled at her son's enthusiasm. Etta's gaze met Mal's. He watched her with an almost painful intensity. Did he wish that it was she on the stool, with their babe in her arms? None of the birthings she'd witnessed before today had moved her, but now Etta found herself wishing to have a child. Mal's child.

The moment passed, and Viola handed the now-full infant to his father, who tucked the other babe into his free arm. Mal and Muireall helped Viola rise and go to the bed. Once she'd settled, Ian passed her their daughter to suckle.

Etta assisted Cecily with scrubbing away the mess of birth. When they finished, Etta hoisted a pan filled with dirty cloths and handed it off to a maid to be laundered. She turned back and found Cecily watching her with a contemplative expression.

"You did well." The older woman's hazel eyes were soft now, and to Etta's astonishment, a slight smile ticked up the edge of her lips. "Here, and at the cairn."

"Thank you." Etta smiled back, but it was still a wary smile, uncertain. "I will never hurt your children, or try to take what is theirs."

"I have never worried that you would take anything from my children," Cecily said. She gestured around at the room. "Their lives are their own, and I have assured their worldly comfort and status as best I could. But hurt?" For a moment, the hard, cold glint returned to her gaze. "Yes, you could hurt them."

"I wouldn't…"

"You're young, dear, and still think that intention matters more than results. But some day, you will comprehend that the world cares little for what you meant to do. It cares only for what happens because of your actions."

Etta swallowed. The words were a rebuke, but not an unjust one. Hadn't she observed that truth, time and again, in the mountains? A man might hunt for days, hoping to feed his family, and yet come home without a single hare or fowl.

"Is it enough that I will do my best not to harm them? That I love them? That they are already a part of me, especially your son?"

"Perhaps." Cecily sighed. "I hope so."

At that, Mal wandered over and took Etta's hand. "Let's leave the new family alone to settle."

"You two should rest," Cecily said. "Especially Etta. She pulled the spirit stone from the cairn this afternoon."

Mal stared at her. "Did you? Is that what—"

"Malcolm." His mother's voice broke through his questions. "See Miss Etta back to her room, please."

Etta's heart squeezed. That was the first time Cecily had used her first name. Yes, she'd shoved "Miss" in front of it, but Etta would wear that down eventually, too.

Out in the hall, Mal did not head left, toward her room, but right. He stopped only a few rooms away, flung open the door, and ushered her inside. The walls were paneled in woods of various stains, creating a pattern of warmth. In the center stood a big bed with heavy drapes hanging from the posters. Mal pulled her past a little desk and a large stuffed chair, flung open one of the drapes, and pushed her into the bed.

"You mother said my room." Etta's tone was only mock-stern, and she loved the way Mal scowled at her as he crawled on top of her.

"Not tonight. In fact, I plan to persuade you never to leave this room again."

He kissed her.

12

20 July 1890

Etta has taken her first lover, although I do not think that it is Love. He's a good boy, and she says that their time together is sweet. I am glad for her. She promises me that she is taking the herbs, and I know she would not forget. She is such a responsible girl. I wish I could have shown her the spell that Gran tried to teach me when I took my first lover, the one that turns sexual energy into magical renewal, but it never worked for me. I found my own way. Perhaps Etta will, as well.

-from the Journal of Aileana Fay Cook

E tta pressed up into Mal's kiss, opening her mouth and twining her tongue with his. She shouldn't do this—shouldn't abuse the fragile connection she'd built with Cecily—but the blood-unity spell still tingled inside of her, and she ached to join her flesh, her magic, to Mal's.

She opened her eyes and her Sight, and deliberately

pressed along the lines of the spell-net that still twined around them, imagining a pair of shears clipping any outside threads that might telegraph their lovemaking to the rest of the family. She didn't know what to do with the cut ends, so she wove them back into the remaining spell, like she would the loose yarn at the end of a knit scarf. The new, separate spell created a cocoon of connection around her and Mal.

Their magic had been batted back and forth between them like a tennis ball today, but now they deliberately joined their gifts, meshing their senses and deepening the connection begun by the unity spell.

I want you so much. Etta arched her hips, grinding her sex against his.

Pleasure spiked, and Mal grinned. He licked from her jaw to the base of her neck and the little hollow there. Her skin tingled and heat shot down into her core. He dragged his tongue back up, shifting sideways to her earlobe, and nipped at the bottom edge.

Etta moaned and bit Mal's shoulder, tugging him close with her hands around his chest and her legs around his hips. He chuckled, and their mouths met again, hungry and open. Etta yanked at the open collar of his shirt and growled when the buttons refused to yield to her frantic fingers.

Mal kissed her again, and pulled away a little. He'd long ago discarded everything but his shirt and trousers, and the cuffs of his shirt had been opened and rolled up, so it took him only a moment to open three buttons and strip it over his head. Etta attacked the thin undershirt, dragging it off so that she could stroke the soft skin of his chest, tickling her fingers over his light sprinkling of hair, then cupping his pectorals, her hands eager for the heat and weight of him under her fingertips. She tantalized them both by teasing her palms over his nipples until they formed tiny peaks that tickled her flesh.

Mal growled, and turned his attention to the buttons down the back of her gown. Her clothes required a frustrating amount of time to divest, but with some curses and chortles, they managed the chore. He left her chemise, trailing his fingers over the thin cotton until she gasped and arched and begged him to take it off.

He took his time, tugging it inch by tantalizing inch up her thighs and over her hips, leaving wet kisses on the skin revealed. He laved his tongue over the rounded flesh of her lower belly and dipped into her navel, making her giggle. When he slid up her ribcage and captured a nipple between his lips, the giggle turned to a moan.

"Harder." She made the demand without shame, and he nearly growled as he suckled her, then dragged his teeth over the tip. "Yes!" she cried, pleasure and heat piercing through her, centering low, between her legs, where she already dripped and ached for him.

He abandoned that breast for the other, nipping the already tight peak between his teeth—almost painfully—and she arched hard against him, clutching at his head, then his back, searching for his trousers. She had to get them off, had to feel him, hot and hard in her hands.

She pushed him, and he went, rolling onto his back. Etta straddled his knees and worked the buttons of his fall, pushing fabric aside until the prize she sought filled her grasp. She gentled her touch, stroking the foreskin away from the soft and sensitive tip, and reveled in his gasps. Her tongue dragged over him from balls to head. A little bead of salty seed had formed there, and she lapped at it, tasting the glorious mix of citrus-magic and musky male. She pressed her lips onto the rounded crown and slowly let them part, taking his cock in her mouth.

"Oh, gods," Mal groaned, and his hips bucked beneath her, trying to force himself deeper inside. Etta closed her hands over the parts of him that didn't fit past her jaws and began to move. She rose and fell, twisting her grip on his shaft, dragging her tongue along the sensitive underside, until he growled at her and pushed her off of him.

He shucked off his trousers and yanked her back to kiss her, a furious meeting of tongues and teeth. *I need to be inside you.* The plea would have been ragged if it had been spoken aloud, but the words had even more impact in her thoughts as his desperation met and resonated with hers.

I need you there. She kissed him back, matching his urgency and clutching at his shoulders. Then she sat up, rubbing her cunny against his lower belly, and took his hand to press it against the wet folds of her sex. *Touch me,* she begged.

He slipped a finger inside of her, and drew out the moisture to slide over her clit. She bucked against his hand, pleasure swamping her with every stroke.

"Now, Etta. It has to be now."

"Yes." She lifted onto her knees, grasped his length, and positioned him at the entrance to her hot, wet core. Then she relaxed, and he slid into her.

"Oh, fuck, love, you're so tight." Mal's voice was low and guttural. His hands on her hips trembled, and the intensity in his blue gaze raised every hair on her body.

Warmth flooded through Etta as she took him inside. She moaned, loving how he stretched her—filled her—her body yielding and swallowing him whole, until his balls rested against her folds.

Etta squeezed her internal muscles to watch Mal gasp and shudder. Then she gave in to his desires and her own, lifting her hips, sliding up his length, and squeezing him as she sank back down. She ground her clitoris against his hipbone, rose, and then lowered to pleasure herself again. And again. And again, until she couldn't maintain the languid pace and instead rode him hard and fast, pulsing around him and against him. The ecstasy built and spiraled inside her, then broke, with a burst of heat and magic. Everything smelled of lemons—of Mal—and her body shook with each bright spike of pleasure until she collapsed, shuddering and spent, on his chest.

When she regained a sense of herself, he was stroking her hair with one hand and her back with the other. He was still hard inside her, and when she lifted her head to meet his gaze, he thrust up, making her gasp and tighten around him.

"You didn't think it was over, did you?" He chuckled, and sat up. But instead of remaining there, he pushed her backward onto the mattress. She lifted her knees and welcomed the weight of him, now nestled between her legs. He braced his upper body above her, and pressed his still-buried cock even deeper within her. Sensation rippled up from her core, making her heartbeat flutter.

"Of course not." She squeezed his cock with her cunny, and he growled. He nipped at her lower lip, and then turned his attention to her breasts. Her nipples had softened after her climax, but he laved each in turn with his tongue, almost humming with pleasure as they formed taut peaks. He punctuated each lick with a thrust into her cunny. She'd never had a second orgasm so soon, but within moments, the pressure of his hips against her clitoris shifted from pleasure-pain to pure pleasure. The heat rose again, and this time they moved together.

The connection sang through thick ropes of magic that wrapped around and through their bodies. She almost cried out when she saw the pulsing web of power now suffusing them. Every move that they made raised a kind of magical energy she'd never known existed. It pulsed along their nerves, pumped through each artery and vein, poured out of Mal and into her and back, growing stronger and more powerful with every thrust of his body into hers. Her hips rose to meet him, and his head lifted from her breast so that he could stare into her eyes.

She met his gaze and everything else fell away. There was only Mal, and only her. Then there was only one being, striving as one flesh, straining toward and finding a peak of pleasure so intense that every other sense shattered.

~

MAL'S HEAVY BODY PRESSED HER DOWN INTO THE MATTRESS. She'd always liked this part of sex, cradling the body of her lover as he lay spent in her arms, but it was even better now. Mal was hers in a way that no other man had been. Sex had never connected her so deeply to another, had never exhausted her flesh while recharging her magic.

"Your thoughts are so busy," Mal grumbled, and lifted his head.

She grinned. "I suppose yours have fled."

"The best orgasm of my life tends to do that to me."

"The best orgasm of my life stimulated a few cogitations." Etta shifted a bit, and then frowned as Mal began to pull away. He gasped as his sensitive flesh slipped out of hers, and she wished she could have kept him inside her a little longer. Perhaps forever.

This man, for the rest of her life. Fear should have sprung up with that thought, but it didn't. They'd made love, and she hadn't lost herself. Instead, she'd found something greater. Something that lifted her up. Far from clouding her senses with passion or obsession, being with Mal made her thoughts and feelings more clear than they'd ever been.

He rolled off her, and sprawled on his back, flopping one arm over his eyes. She shifted to her side and propped herself on her arm to look at him. He was gorgeous naked. Not so muscular as to be massive, but enough to have defined edges under his pale, freckled skin. She wanted to run her tongue over him, everywhere. Wanted to taste and touch him and mark him as hers. She'd never wanted that before, had never wanted to claim a man she slept with. But she did now.

"Oh, very well. I'm too fuzzy to interpret at the moment." He removed the arm from over his face and blinked at her. "What's going on in your head?"

She slid one leg over his. "I'm thinking about how I'd like to lick you all over."

"Ah." A muscle jumped in his jaw, his blue eyes heated, and the corner of his mouth turned up. "I suppose I could allow it."

"And I was thinking that, perhaps we might…" she trailed off, uncertain how to ask for what she wanted.

"Might what? Do it again, this time standing up? Or with you bent over the bed and me taking you from behind? Because that is a suggestion I'd be happy to assist you with." He levered toward her and ran a hand along her side, from her hip, up her ribs, to the sensitive skin beneath her breast.

"No, that's not what I mean." She grinned. "Although I'm sure we'll get around to trying both of those things." She stroked a finger from the hollow of his throat down his breastbone. "What I meant was that we've done magic together twice today. I know the first time was awful, and I'm still sorry about what happened. But this time was beautiful, and I wanted to maybe try something else."

Mal's hand stilled, his fingertips stopping beside her nipple. Although he hadn't touched it, it pebbled.

He pulled away, and rolled into a sitting position. Fear and shame and anger flooded across the fragile bond of their magic, and she flinched, falling back against the pillows.

"I hadn't realized," he said, then stopped himself. His fists closed around the bedclothes, and he drew his knees close to his chest, as though to protect his heart. "I hadn't thought about what would happen when we made love."

"You mean, that we would cast a spell with our bodies?"

He didn't nod, but his silence was a kind of answer.

"I told you about what happened with Ian and Viola. I didn't tell you that, after that day, I couldn't do magic at all. Everything I tried fell apart. I almost set my lodgings on fire one night trying to light a damned lantern." Shudders wracked his frame, and he wrapped his arms around his knees, his posture stooped and huddled.

Etta wanted to touch him—to comfort him—but she didn't want to call more attention to her presence beside him in the bed, lest he stop talking.

"When I swore never to do magic again, it wasn't only because I hurt Ian and my sister. It was because I broke something in myself."

Words flew out of her—words that attempted to reassure —but even as she spoke them, she knew they would make no difference. "Whatever was wrong then, it isn't wrong now. We've brought our magic together several times, and you were with me when I took out the stone. Your presence didn't make me fail. We created a spell here tonight, in this bed, and the net is still strong. You aren't broken."

She gestured at the threads of the unity spell, still surrounding and infusing them. New layers criss-crossed the old, each strand intricate and beautiful, forming a magical representation of their lovemaking.

Mal stared at it in horror. "I had no idea we were doing that. Gods, Etta. I could have killed us both, or ripped the magic right out of us."

Her patience and compassion were rapidly wearing thin. "You didn't. You wouldn't."

"I could have. You don't know—"

"Stop being so melodramatic." She rose to her knees and

leaned over him. "Something bad happened to you. You needed time to get over it, to grieve and heal. Now it's done, and I'm here. We'll figure it out together."

She stared into his eyes, so blue and wide, like a summer sky over the Roan. Then they closed, and he lowered his chin to his chest.

"I can't. You need to be here, with my family. You need my mother and Aunt Muireall to teach you." He opened his eyes again, and a new fervor shone out of him and through their bond. "I'm going back to my estate, where it's safe. As long as I'm with you, your magic and mine will seek to meld, and we've already seen how much that can hurt. I'll explain things to my mother. She'll make my father understand."

"We're melded right now, Malcolm. It doesn't hurt." Her voice came out low, and soft, and he flinched. "If you're trying to invent excuses for why you don't want to be with me..." she trailed off, her own fear now flooding their bond. Until tonight, she'd been afraid that love would overwhelm her. That she'd become obsessed with Mal, and him with her, as her mother and father had with each other.

And then, for one brief and gorgeous moment, the fear had vanished. She'd believed she'd found her complement, the harmony to her melody. Mal was her match, not someone who would subsume her, or make her lose sight of herself.

She had never considered that he would be all of those things to her, but not want them in return.

Etta slashed through the unity spell, and the extra layers that she and Mal had wrought. She didn't rip her magic away from his—she didn't want to hurt him even though she was furious with him. She pulled her magic away carefully, the way he'd shown her, untangling the mesh that didn't want to come undone.

"Wait," he said, but she'd already extricated her magic, and flung herself off the bed.

"I do want you, Etta. More than I've ever wanted anything." He crawled after her, and stood while she searched the floor for her clothes.

"You must not have wanted anything much, then." She kicked his trousers out of the way.

He didn't come to her, didn't interfere. Didn't contradict her. "I can't have you. I can't risk you."

She found her shift, and tugged it on. That would have to do for now. She couldn't spare the time to don the other necessary layers.

"You mean you can't risk yourself. Well, fine. That's lovely. Your mother will be thrilled."

He stood there beside the bed, naked and glorious, his frown a picture of frustration. "No, that's not it at all. You can't appreciate it, because magic is so new to you. It's all about discovery and wonder." He lifted his hands, both of them curled into tight fists. "I can't feel that anymore. And I can't be with you when every time you do magic, I flinch in pain." Both fists jabbed back down to his sides, and it was Etta who flinched. But not from fear. From anger.

"I won't renounce my magic for you, and I won't run away from this family. I've just found them. I'm not giving them up." But if he asked her to...would she? Oh, Great Mother. Would she? She understood, now, her mother's temptation. How she'd made choice after choice to stay with her husband, to live the life he chose—the life he needed—rather than the life that would have been best for her. That would have been best for their daughter. After all these years, Etta finally comprehended the pull of one man's love on a woman.

Mal didn't ask. "Even if you did come with me, you couldn't forsake your magic. Like Aunt Muireall said in Glasgow, it's riding you, and it isn't going to stop because you deny it. You have to learn." His gaze fell, as if he couldn't bear to look at her anymore. He shifted, angling his body back toward the bed. Something twisted in her gut, and warmth spiked up through her chest, gathering behind her eyes like a dark cloud threatening rain. His head lowered and his chin touched his shoulder, hiding his face from her. "I can't be a part of that."

"Then don't." She spat the words at him as the warmth inside turned to burning pain. She wrapped her arms around her bundle of clothes and stalked out into the corridor. Thank the gods that Ian and Viola had put her in the family wing. If she'd had to climb more stairs, had to risk being seen, she would have been mortified.

Great Mother, she'd never been ashamed of taking a lover before. The hot ache curdled in her chest, catching in her lungs. She swallowed a sob, hunching inward and clutching her bundle against her ribs.

She made it to her room and slammed the door. She dropped her clothes to the floor, flung herself into the bed, and—for the first time since she'd left America—wept.

MILES TO THE NORTHWEST, IN A LITTLE FISHING VILLAGE ON the Isle of Skye, Amelia finished forming the final threads of a spell. She'd been weaving it for days, laying a trail as she traveled parallel to the Fays from Glasgow, and then out to sea. The family tossed so much magic around, no one noticed a few extra threads here and there. Certainly not Etta, who wouldn't know the difference between a deliberate brush of a spell and the natural spikes of power in the Highlands.

Now, those carefully laid nets would trap Amelia's prey.

She reached out along her spell. Her power stretched across land and sea, over lochs and rivers and mountains, until it came to rest at Emberlach, and into the sleeping mind of Etta Mae Cook.

Amelia breathed the words that would plant her vision into Etta's mind.

The spell blossomed, and even from this distance, Amelia felt Etta shiver. She'd crafted the dream with exquisite care. It utilized everything she'd learned about the little American witch, from the reports she'd received from her spies in Raleigh, to their last meeting on the train to Glasgow.

Amelia had every confidence that when Miss Cook awoke, she would make her way to Skye. Alone.

13

22 February 1893

It is five years today that Fayt died. Five years with part of my heart ripped from my chest. I miss him like fury and thunder, like parched earth longing for rain. But I see our Etta, casting minor spells that look more like his mother's work than mine—the pittance that I was able to show her—and I know that part of him is still here. Part of us both lives on in our daughter. Flesh of our flesh. Blood of our blood.

It is my blood in her I worry about. There was an Englishman in Bakersville last week, who had a small but not insignificant talent. Etta was instantly infatuated with his rolling vowels and clipped consonants. With his tailored clothes and polished manners. Thank the Great Spirit he left as quickly as he'd arrived.

-from the journal of Aileana Fay Cook

Etta struggled up from sleep, a scream barely stifled in her throat. The room was dark, and her eyes felt puffy and sore from weeping. She couldn't have been asleep for long. The fire had gone out, and cold air cascaded over her as she pushed off her blankets. She had to hurry.

She'd only had a few visions before, and nothing had ever been as clear as this. Danger, coming to Clan Fay. The house on Skye had been the source, or maybe the epicenter of the threat.

The vision had shown her what she had to do and where she had to go. If she failed, the clan would be shattered. If she did not go alone, Mal would die.

Etta stumbled over to the wardrobe, where Beth had hung her dresses. She pulled out two of the plainer gowns— made of cotton and wool—that fit her without a corset. She threw them onto the chair by the dressing table. Beth had tucked her valise inside a chest at the foot of the bed, along with her boots, undergarments, and—thank the Great Mother—her trousers.

She dressed quickly in trousers, boots, and one of the dresses. She stuffed everything else into the valise, including the small pouch of money that she'd exchanged in Portsmouth but had not yet required.

The big clock in the hall chimed a quarter past three in the morning. She found the servants' door hidden in the wall beside the clock and followed the side passage to the kitchens, then outside.

The horses shifted and huffed in the darkened stables. She'd inherited a touch of her father's ability with animals and was a good rider, though she preferred riding a horse she'd had time to get to know. *Needs must when the dark god drives.*

She did not open her Sight to check for active magic. Instead, she followed her magical instincts, letting them guide her to a horse that might be willing to let an unfamiliar human guide it out into a summer's night.

At the end of the row, a mare poked her head over her door. That one would do.

Etta saddled the horse and rode down the main road to the village. She arrived in the pale grey gloaming before dawn. A few coins exchanged hands and a local fisherman agreed to take her on his boat. His son led the horse to the inn's stable.

With that, she was on her way to Skye.

MAL WOKE WITH A POUNDING HEADACHE AND A SOUR TASTE IN his mouth. He rolled over and pushed his forehead into the pillow, hoping the pressure would ease some of the pain in his skull. No such luck.

He ought to have woken energized and refreshed. Every other time he'd been part of the blood-unity spell, he'd felt blissful for weeks afterward. Not this time.

No, this time he'd raised a large amount of sexual energy with the woman he'd loved, and then had panicked and shoved all the extra power back at her. Then he'd topped off his idiocy by drinking the better part of a bottle of single malt he'd meant to use to toast the new bairns with Ian.

Instead of fresh and full, he was drained and empty, as though he'd helped his tenants through shearing season again and gotten knocked about the head by a few rams.

He stumbled out of bed and over to his washstand. The water was tepid, but he splashed it on his face anyway, and made a mental note to put a bee in his father's ear about hot, running water at Emberlach.

The mirror over the basin revealed bloodshot eyes, sickly pale skin, and a scruffy jawline. He rubbed at his chin. What a mess he was. What a mess he had made.

A knock at the door had his head throbbing again. Well, had his head throbbing more, since it hadn't stopped yet.

He was more-or-less decently covered in the nightshirt he'd donned after Etta left, so he yelled, "Come in!"

If he'd known his mother was at the door, he'd have put on his dressing gown first. As it was, he stood before her, hair disheveled, face covered in stubble, and bare from the thigh down. This day was not going well.

She glanced around the room, and back at him in all his unkempt glory. Then she shocked him. "I expected to find Miss Etta here with you." And she didn't look unhappy about that. What divergent plane had he awoken on this morning?

"She's not." *I was an ass, and I sent her away.* He didn't say those words aloud. Nor did he admit the other thoughts tumbling through his head: *I was terrified, and I told her I couldn't be a part of her life. I'm still too damned afraid to go after her. I'm a fucking coward.*

"But she was." His mother crossed to the bed, where one lone stocking lay, abandoned on the coverlet. Etta must have missed it in her rush to gather her clothes.

There was no point in denying it. His mother knew he didn't sleep with the servants, and no one else in the house was likely to have been in his room taking off her stockings last night. "She was."

Two word sentences appeared to be his limit this morning.

"I had hoped to speak to you both together, but I will give you the news and then we can find her." She clasped her hands together, her features soft and relaxed.

"What news?" He didn't trust that bland look. She'd often

blistered his ears with a scold while wearing that exact same expression.

"Muireall and I conferred after the twins were born, and we've agreed to take Etta on as a student. We do have some minor conditions, but I'll discuss those with her."

Elation flared inside him, and some of his petty anger dissipated. He was truly happy for Etta. This was what she'd wanted, why she'd come to Britain. And he could not begrudge her the chance to use her magic and be at peace.

Fast on the heels of joy came despair. Etta would have what she wanted, and he would lose her. He knew, now, that he could not hope to be in her presence and not be drawn into her magic. He'd found his perfect match, his magical mate, but to be together meant he would be forsworn. She'd already pulled him into a spell. Even if they both warded themselves, it was going to happen again.

He'd hoped, with her, he might eventually find a way back to his magic. But after yesterday—after the spell at the cairn —he knew better. He'd broken under the pressure and had hurt them both. It was the same as before, and if two years hadn't made a difference, how could she?

"That's wonderful." He meant the words, and was glad that Etta would be trained, but his miserable tone must have been clear, too.

"You don't sound pleased. Does her absence have something to do with that?"

"It might." He couldn't meet her gaze, and stared down at the hem of her skirt. It had two sedate ruffles, more lines of pleats than actual ruffles. Just like his mother's magic, present but subdued.

"Did you tell her that your vow against doing magic was more important than being with her?"

Mal flinched at her perceptive comment, almost as though she'd read his mind, and pain erupted in his skull from the abrupt movement. His mother hadn't done that since he was a teenager. It wasn't anything magical, either, but some sort of ability that mothers had to divine exactly what went on inside their offspring's minds.

"I did."

"You're a fool, Cuthbert Malcolm Elliott Seward." Ah, the full name treatment. He supposed he deserved that. "Everyone in that room last night felt how strong her connection is to us. She held nothing back in the spell. She did that out of love. For us, yes, but also for you."

Love? She hadn't spoken of love, and neither had he. Connection? Yes. Lust and passion? Gods, yes. But not love. She didn't love him. Did she?

His mother made an exasperated noise in the back of her throat. Mal started. She actually sounded Scottish.

"You're going to go with me to see her, and you're going to give her the good news. You're also going to apologize, and tell her that you'll be training alongside her. Muireall wants you to be her partner, and said that a little time relearning the basics will help you find your way back from where you've been these last two years."

"Mother, I—"

"Allow me to finish, Malcolm." She glared at him, and he leaned back against the washstand. He might as well be a toddler in nappies again. Straightening her shoulders, she continued. "There is something else, and I'm glad you're going to hear it before she does, because you can help me soften the blow."

"The blow?"

"Stop interrupting. You and I might not see it as a blow, but she will." She smoothed out her skirts, and then looked him straight in the eye. "Etta is the Duchess of Fay."

He spluttered. There was nothing dignified about the sounds that came out of his mouth, or the way he stumbled, making the washstand totter. "She's the what?" At last he'd managed more than two words.

She came to him and put her hands on his arms, steadying him. "She's the Duchess of Fay."

He stared at his mother's face, usually so serene, but now almost troubled. "How do you know?"

"Muireall and I suspected based on letters her mother exchanged with Great-Aunt Beatrice and even with Lilias herself over the last two decades. But letters aren't proof, and Etta might have been lying, or brought up to believe a lie." She broke eye contact, and let go of his arms. "Yesterday, she pulled the spirit stone from the cairn, which only a family member accepted by the land could have done. But still, that did not mean she was the duchess." She backed away, and leaned against his bedpost. His mother never leaned. He truly had awoken in some other world.

"The blood-unity spell gave us the final piece. If you know how to look for it, the various symbols and structures of the threads binding each family member into the spell show their lines of descent. Etta's is purely matrilineal, all the way back, as far as the spell can remember."

"And that makes her the Duchess of Fay?"

She sighed, and actually rubbed a hand against her temple and eyebrow. Who was this woman, and what had she done with his always-formal, never emotive mother?

"Lilias required that her Letters Patent be written in the old Scottish style, where matrilineal descent is the qualifier for the title. In fact, she made it so that it cannot be held in abeyance for a generation by a male and then given to one of his daughters. It must pass from daughter-to-daughter. Neither Muireall nor I can ever hold it. It belongs to Etta, and her daughters."

"She's going to hate that." And, though he had not imagined finding any humor in this morning, Mal laughed. His head protested with a bright flash of pain. "Gods, it's just about the worst thing that could have happened to her."

"I am aware of that. But we need her to embrace the title, and everything it means. You are going to have to help with that." She pointed at him, and even from across the room, it felt like a poke to the belly.

"How am I supposed to get her to agree? She's upset with me after I made a cake of myself last night." Mal wiped at his forehead. He'd begun to sweat.

"Let me tell you a secret. A sincere apology, coupled with a genuine desire to change your behavior, will almost always get a woman's attention." Her expression said that she expected him to perform the suggested action immediately.

"I am sincerely sorry. But Mother, I don't know that I can change…what she would need me to change." He scrubbed his face and lowered his head. He rubbed at the bridge of his nose.

"You mean you can't overcome your fear of doing active spells overnight?"

He'd almost closed his eyes, but his eyelids fluttered open and his hand dropped to his side. "Er, yes." Back to two-word answers.

"She is a reasonable person. She won't expect you to become a magical paragon immediately following your apology. Ask her for time, and she will give it."

"What if it doesn't work? What if I can never do magic again?"

"You will. And it's time you believed that."

Mal sucked in a breath. The room brimmed with magic, the remnants of the power he and Etta had raised together last night. Etta's deep-woods scent and the richness of tilled earth, combined with his own lemony-citrus, woke fresh desire inside him. Yes, the cairn spell had been awful. But when they made love—when he had allowed the magic to flow through him naturally—it had been amazing.

He wanted to believe his mother, wanted to grab at any future that gave him both magic and Etta. "All right. Let's go talk to her."

He picked up his trousers from where they lay crumpled on the floor and pulled them on. He'd managed to locate his shirt by the time Sorcha stuck her head in his open door.

"There's a problem."

His hands fisted. It could be any sort of problem, from one of the new water closets overflowing to the twins already developing colic. But it wasn't. He knew before Sorcha said the words, knew the moment he searched with his magic and detected only echoes where he should have found his lover.

"Etta is gone."

~

THE ADULT MEMBERS OF THE CLAN—MINUS THE NEW PARENTS, who had been awake all night feeding and caring for their newborn twins—gathered in the big dining room around the long table. Aunt Muireall and Mother sat at one end, with Sorcha on one side, and Mal on the other. Mal hadn't thought the problem required a full clan meeting, but Mother had disagreed. Now, she had Sorcha present the family with the facts as they knew them.

"Before I left Fay House, I had a vision of Etta coming to Skye. I meant to warn her not to go yet, but I didn't believe it was urgent. Everyone is here, and she'd have no reason to go without one of us along."

"What's the danger?" Uncle Robert asked.

Sorcha frowned. "I don't know, exactly. It wasn't a specific kind of vision, more of the vague type that hints at disaster but does not give details. Still, I knew she wasn't to go yet, and must not go at all until after midsummer."

"Which is today," Robert said. "It would take her three days by boat to get there, and from what the villagers told Neill, she convinced old Dougal MacClaren to take her out to Loch Linnhe."

Uncle Neill chimed in. "If she goes up to Fort William, she could get on a horse and be at Mullaig by sundown, ready to take the ferry to Skye."

"It's pointless to speculate," Muireall said. "Now that we're all together, I will scry for her."

One of her daughters stepped away from the far wall, carrying a shallow bronze bowl. The other daughter held a clay pitcher. The pitcher would be full of spring water, freshly drawn.

Seonag placed the bowl in front of her mother, and Ainsley poured the water. Muireall took Sorcha and his mother's hands. Everyone else at the table grasped their neighbor's hands as well, until they were linked in a long oval. Mal wished he had a better view of the scrying bowl, but waited to hear Muireall's pronouncement.

Time stretched out, like taffy pulled from its wrapper, getting thinner and thinner without ever breaking loose. Scrying did not require active magic, only an understanding of how energy flowed and the ability to open one's mind to the infinite. Mal understood this, but hated every moment wasted while Muireall communed with the essence of magic.

"She went by water."

Everyone at the table released their breath, a shared exhalation that might have made Mal laugh, if he didn't want to leap up and follow Etta.

"So the worst disaster is already averted," Mal said. "We'll go by land and prevent her from getting to Fay House. I'll saddle some horses and we can ride for Fort William."

His mother squeezed his hand. "It isn't that simple, Malcolm. Sorcha, tell them the rest."

Sorcha let go of Muireall's hand. "I had another vision last night. This one isn't about what happens if Etta goes to Skye. It's about what happens if we try to stop her."

"What does that mean?" He should have kept his mouth shut and let her finish, but the words burst out of him.

"It means if we stop Etta now, we may never discover who is leeching magic from Britain. I don't know how, but Etta going to Skye is somehow tied to the search. The vision I had felt like one of Lilias's teaching dreams, almost as though she were giving me the warning herself."

"So if she goes, she's in danger," Muireall said, "or Fay House is. But if she doesn't go, British magic will die."

Sorcha nodded. "Yes. And to be clear, I truly do not know if the danger she faces is for her, for our land, or for us as a clan. But the danger to magic was certain. I feel it unwise to stop her now."

"What about helping her?"

Bless Mother for asking the question that clamored inside him.

"I don't know." Sorcha frowned, and pressed a hand against her belly. "When I thought about going myself, I nearly vomited. That's how strong the aversion was. So I don't believe it's a good idea."

"I won't accept that." Mal banged his fist on the tabletop. "You can't let her go into danger alone, when one of you could help."

Sorcha met his gaze across the table. Under her pale brows, her eyes looked like a summer sky. "The idea of you going, Mal, doesn't make me ill. Anyone else, yes, but not you."

Every part of him stilled, to the core of his being. Because he knew what she meant, and the truth of her words pierced his objections like a spear. He was the only one. No one else could do this. No one else had the connection with her, or the trust, or—gods damn it—the love.

But could he do what was required? Could he trust *himself* to not falter when she needed him most?

He'd walked away from this family—from the clan—when he'd caused Viola's magic to be ripped apart. He would not have come back if his mother hadn't forced him to, and if he hadn't been so enamored with Etta that he barely noticed anyone else.

He looked around the table. Last night, they'd been wary of him. After what happened at Viola's wedding, he couldn't blame them. But the blood-unity spell had been cast, and he'd not interfered. More, he'd participated, like everyone else.

Now he understood that they hadn't been wary because they thought he was going to actively hurt someone else. They worried that his negative attitude would spoil the spell, and that the new bairns would be born into discord instead of harmony.

Did no one care about what he'd done to his sister? Or was Viola correct, and no one actually blamed him?

Did it matter, as long as he still blamed himself? "What if I make things worse?"

A familiar magic pressed against him, its jagged missing piece ripping at his heart.

Viola spoke from the doorway. "You didn't make Ian cast that spell, Malcolm. He knew it was too much for him. Did he never tell you that? He knew, and he did it anyway, because I'd goaded him. But that doesn't mean I'm any more responsible than you, or him. We all made bad decisions that day, and we have all paid the price for them." Her words made him look deeper, underneath the torn edge, to where her power and her soul pulsed and hummed.

She limped into the room, her gait unsteady. Ian walked beside her, his arm steadying her. His magic joined hers, and that jagged corner filled. Both of them lit with joy, and Viola's familiar summer-storm scent mixed with Ian's immutable stone, becoming the very familiar aroma of the Highlands under a rainy sky. They'd truly merged their magic, had become one in a way that Mal had never believed possible.

"We've accepted what happened, Mal," Ian said. "It's time you did, too. Time to move on, for all of us."

Mal twisted in his chair to follow their progress toward him. "I don't know that I can."

A hand came to rest on his shoulder. Mother's hand. "Of course you can, my love."

He snapped back around, and stared. She'd never done that before, had never used an endearment in a place where others could hear. And now she'd done it in front of the entire family.

"We can't go with you," Sorcha said, "but we are all behind you. You must do this. You are the only one of us who can."

Magic swamped over him—wave after wave—from Viola and Ian, his mother, Muireall, Sorcha, and all the rest. Etta needed him, and Clan Fay supported him.

He did not yet believe, but he would try.

14

1 October 1893

I dreamed of Gran last night. She was a young girl in the dream, no older than ten, sitting on the edge of a cliff with two young women, who were clearly her sisters. The oldest one scolded her for using made-up spells, and she countered that their mother made up magic all the time, so why couldn't she?

Was it just a dream, or was it a memory? I have often thought to tell Etta to experiment with her gift. It was, after all, how I learned. But my magic rewards intuition and instinct. Etta's is built around rules and strictures.

Perhaps I should not focus on Gran's words, but her sister's. And yet...I cannot send Etta away. I can't bear to lose her, too.

-from the journal of Aileana Fay Cook

The cliffs below Fay House glowed with afternoon light. Etta watched them grow larger from her perch in the bow of yet another fisherman's boat. She'd traveled on a variety of crafts since her journey began, from a trim little sailing ketch, to a steam-powered ferryboat. This was the smallest yet, but it was quick, and she hadn't had many other choices. No one else would agree to sail her around from Armadale to the Fay land, near Glenbrittle.

The fisherman's accent was so thick as to be nearly impenetrable, but she understood enough to catch that their destination was ahead. She thought what he said was, "There's the house there, at the top of that rise," but any number of those words could have been different. Perhaps they were still miles away.

But no. He shifted the tiller, and the boat skimmed out of the deeper waters and in toward the little cove at the base of the cliffs. He couldn't get her all the way to shore without oars to fight against the surf, but she thanked him, hefted her pack, and leapt over the side.

The water was cold, the waves choppy. She could swim, but she'd never fought the ocean before. She'd put her boots in the pack and went barefoot at the fisherman's pantomimed suggestion, and she praised his foresight as she kicked against the current that caught in her skirts, saltwater slapping at her face and driving up her nostrils.

Soon she reached a point where the waves pushed her toward the beach, and a few minutes later she climbed out onto a mix of rock and sand.

She turned and waved at the fisherman, who waved back. She'd told him not to wait, and he didn't. He sailed off to take her coin back to Armadale, a just compensation for the lack of a day's catch.

The beach was small, and roughly circular, with a little

dip in the cliffs at the center. A path climbed from the shore-line. Etta took the path, dripping, and hoped there were servants at the house who could provide her with some dry clothing and a place to wash. Sharp rocks bit into her tender feet, and twice she considered trying to wrestle on her wet boots.

When she gained the top of the cliffs, she stopped caring about wet clothes, boots, or rocks.

At her first sight of Fay House, magic pummeled out of the earth beneath her, slamming into her like a runaway carriage against a tree. She gasped and staggered, her body convulsing, as she tried to find enough breath to scream.

AMELIA SAT IN A SHELTERED SPOT OF THE FAY HOUSE gardens, watching the cliff path. Etta should arrive soon.

She reviewed what she would say, how she would present her case. The Fay clan was hiding things from Etta. They didn't want her to know that she was the next duchess—that she could take over the clan if she wanted. Muireall and Cecily were afraid of her. They would never train her like she wanted. They would keep her away from the family, because they didn't want to lose their power.

That was good. Play against her fear of being alone, and push at her need to belong. Then offer the queen as an alter-native, and the queen's ladies as a new magical family.

Yes. That would work.

Hoofbeats sounded in the distance, coming from the direction of town. A rider? She'd convinced the servants she was a friend of the family by providing a forged letter from Cecily. But they hadn't been expecting any other visitors—she'd asked. So who was coming?

Amelia stood and strode toward the house. She made it

around to the drive in time to see Malcolm Seward, Cecily's son, leaping off a sweating horse.

That was when all the hells broke loose.

~

What should have been barely more than a day's journey had turned to three. His horse had thrown a shoe outside Glenfinnan, and the blacksmith had been away from the forge for a two day visit. He'd eventually negotiated the trade of his horse for another, but the delay had cost him six hours. That meant he had to stay overnight in the town, and then he hadn't arrived at Mullaig and the ferry until near dark the next night. He'd managed the crossing this morning, and found that Etta had sailed at first light. He used the Fay name to coerce the ferryman to take the much quicker steam-powered ferryboat around to Fay Village, the closest port to Fay House, but then he had a twenty-minute ride to get to the house proper.

He didn't know if he'd make it first, and he'd hoped to have some time to scout the property before she arrived. He pressed his horse hard, keeping to a canter, accepting the jarring of his bones as penance for pushing Etta away in the first place.

If they'd been together, they could have talked about whatever she'd seen that made her run to Skye. They could have gone to Sorcha, or his mother, or Muireall. He was the world's biggest fool.

Finally he crested a hill, and saw Fay House on the other side. He nudged his mount to a gallop, and they flew down the drive to the sprawling stone building. It wasn't quite a castle, or a manor house of a particular style, or any easily identifiable structure. It had been a castle originally, and then, briefly, a palace, and then a ruin, before the modern incarnation of the Fay family built the first part of the House from the old structure's bones. So much had been added since then that the place was a jumbled amalgam of several hundred years' worth of architectural styles.

The whimsy and the wonder of it had always fascinated him as a child, but now all he wanted was to get there, and get off his horse, and find Etta.

The horse's hooves pounded up the road, to the front of the house, and Mal threw himself out of the saddle almost before the poor thing stopped. A startled servant waited on the drive, and Mal tossed the reins in his direction before stalking off, toward the sea.

He could feel her, there, and every magical instinct in his body shouted that whatever Sorcha had seen, it was about to happen.

AMELIA HAD NEVER FELT POWER LIKE THIS, HAD NEVER dreamed that so much could be held in one place. It erupted from some well deep within the ground, ripping through the surface, and away. Everything shook and trembled. She fell to her knees and then managed to stand again, wobbling toward the cliffs.

Etta stood at the top of the path, the lightning rod for the surge of power, her arms rigid and outstretched, convulsing as the energy poured into her body. It had suffused her so fully that it literally burst from her skin in shafts of light. How was the girl doing this? How had she summoned so much power?

How had the Fays hidden such a rich source beneath their land for so long without the queen finding out? This went beyond defying Her Majesty's wishes and teaching practical magic in their little Scottish school. This much power belonged only in the hands of the monarch, not some upstart American girl.

Another upheaval knocked Amelia over. She crawled toward Etta, and stretched out with her magic. She didn't know what she would do, beyond a vague notion of redirecting the energy away from Etta, but the moment she tried, the power reacted.

Something like an invisible hand, or tendril, wrapped around her, lifting her from the earth, and dragging her toward the cliffs.

Then she was falling, and dark water rushed to meet her.

MAL RAN, FASTER THAN HIS FEET HAD EVER TAKEN HIM, stumbling over the heaving ground, until he reached Etta's side. She was screaming—he could hear it in his mind—but no sound came out of her mouth.

Above her, clouds began to gather. They swirled, darkening even as Mal watched, until they were black, blocking out the sky. Lightning flickered and the wind rose to a keening, violent pitch. Thunder shook the air.

What was he supposed to do? How could anyone control such power? This was Ian and Viola all over again, except thousands of times worse. Another spell gone out of control, and no way for him to stop it.

Or was there? With Ian, they had not been linked. If they had, Mal could have helped shoulder some of Ian's burden. But they hadn't, and so Viola had stepped in, bolstering Ian's magic and losing her own in the process.

Now, it was Etta who needed assistance. Could he do as Viola had done? Could he share his strength with her, and more, his knowledge? She held so much raw energy within herself, and it had to go somewhere, anywhere else. The only spells she knew were simple ones that would never hold such incredible forces.

Mal knew many spells, including some Lilias had shown him that he would never have been able to cast without the entire clan linked together. There was one, in particular, that he had never even dreamed of trying, one that there was no good reason for her to have taught him.

Lilias was a canny old bird, and she must have foreseen this moment, when her heir came home, and was almost overwhelmed by the power the duchess had stored over a hundred years.

Damn it. He had to try.

Mal threw himself at Etta, and latched his mouth onto hers.

Their magic merged, seamless and perfect, as it had every time since that night in Glasgow.

You must do what I do, Etta. It's the only way we survive this.

I can't! She won't let me!

She? Mal dropped into the lower levels of Etta's consciousness, to the point where the magic of Fay House had latched onto his love. And there was, indeed, a *she* there. Lilias. He knew her magic, knew the feel of her spells, remembered the distinctive shape of her threads. What was this?

The spell was tied so deeply into Etta's magic that it had become part of it, a symbiont that had fully mimicked the structure and shape of its host. The only kind of spell that did that was illegal, but was one that Lilias had created during her time on the continent, fighting Napoleon. It was a type of coercion called a geas, and somehow, Lilias had managed to cast it on her great-great-granddaughter.

Mal traveled the tendrils of the geas with his magical senses, trying to discern its purpose. He had to delve deep, through layers of weaving, to the core spell. And there, he heard Lilias's voice again. But it was not the raspy sound of an elderly witch, as he'd known her. No, this was a young woman, not much more than a girl. How was this possible? And she'd been so strong, already.

"Forgive me, daughter of my line." That voice said. *"I lay this geas upon you, and your heirs. Find out what is stealing magic from the British Isles. And, if you can, steal it back."*

Damn her and her quixotic mission. The magic of Fay House thundered through Etta, through the geas, through him, ready to assist the remnants of Lilias in the one purpose that had defined her life.

Etta, I know what to do. Follow me, love. Let go, and I will lead.

Even her internal voice was gone, but with the little self-will she had remaining, she gave herself over to him.

Back in his physical body, he raised his arms. Etta's lifted, too, fingers outstretched, and Mal froze. She was at his mercy, and he had not completed a spell in over two years. This was the most ambitious thing he'd ever tried, and the woman he loved might die if he made a mistake.

His muscles trembled, and his gut clenched. Heat and nausea wrapped around his abdomen.

He must do this. If he tried, he might fail. But if he did nothing, she would surely die, and take this portion of Skye with her.

His right hand swooped, gathering a thread of power as thick as his wrist in its wake. Etta moved with him, and, as one, they crafted the net of a spell.

Each subsequent thread pulled more power out of Etta, and into the weaving. As the force of magic drained out of her, she came more and more back to herself, but still she did not speak.

He acted for both of them, spoke the words of the spell for his voice and hers, and then it was done.

Light and heat and pressure shot out of the net, and then

coalesced back, shrinking and sinking into the earth. The spell moved deeper into the bedrock below the house, and then stopped.

The old lines of power, so familiar to his senses from yearly visits to this spot, began to shift, aligning to the new node that he and Etta had created.

How did you know that would work?

It wasn't what he wanted to talk about, but if she needed to ask, he would answer.

I didn't. But Lilias taught me that spell when I was far too young to use it, and she must have had a reason. When I realized whose voice was inside that geas, I knew that she'd planned all of this. I hate her for that, for using you.

For using us. She lifted a hand, her movements once again distinct from his, and touched his cheek. *If it hadn't been for you, Mal, I wouldn't have been able to control it. I almost didn't. I was almost...not me, anymore.* Her hand began to shake, and he captured it in his.

That didn't happen. You're still my Etta.

"Get away from her!"

Mal was so startled to hear another voice that he actually did as he was commanded.

That was a mistake. He and Etta were both drained, and the newcomer was not. Magical force slammed into him, knocking him aside and at least fifteen feet away. He landed on his outstretched arm, and something snapped.

Agony pulsed out of his forearm, and his connection to Etta broke under the stabbing pressure.

He sat up, pain coursing through him, and stared at the new tableau by the edge of the cliff. Lady Falcestershire—dripping and cross, and despite that looking every inch the Queen's Sorceress—had Etta wrapped in a tight net of air. Etta's head lolled to one side. Had the force of the restraints snapped her neck?

But then her face lifted above the spell net, and she turned to face Lady Falcestershire. Relief flooded him.

"What are you doing here?" Etta asked.

"I brought you here." Lady Falcestershire's fingers twitched, and the spell holding Etta tightened.

"You? Then the vision—"

"A spell. But I had no idea that this would happen. What was that power? How did it get here?" She shook Etta, using the spell. Mal tried to go to them, to get Etta away from her, but bright, sharp pain lanced through him, and he nearly vomited.

"I have no idea." Etta struggled against the bonds, but the only thing that moved was her shoulders, head, and feet. "You know I've never been here before."

"How did you channel it?" Lady Falcestershire demanded. She was fully in her guise as the magical hand of the queen now, power and authority radiating from her in its own, inexorable kind of magic. "How did it not destroy you, and everything around you?"

"I couldn't. I didn't. I don't know..." Etta trailed off, and Mal needed to get to her. Needed to comfort her, to explain what happened and why, to quiet the voice of their long-dead great-grandmother that was probably still screaming in her head.

He managed to get back to his feet and cradled his broken arm against his chest. He lurched forward, but Lady Falcestershire held up a hand. On her finger a ring glittered, the ring that marked her as the highest mage in England. It was also, if his mother's speculation was correct, a powerful magical talisman in its own right. Mal stopped.

"I can't allow this act to go unpunished. You have both violated the fundamental use of magic laws, but as Malcolm is a member of Clan Fay, he'll have to go to his clan chief for punishment. You, Etta, will go to the queen." She drew her tiny shoulders back and raised the other hand. Threads of power formed around her dancing fingers. "As Her Majesty's lawful representative, I bind you, Etta Mae Cook, to appear before the queen at Balmoral. You will come with me now."

Mal found the will to limp forward. "Not a chance. You're not taking her away with you."

Etta tilted her head to look at him, and there was something shattered and awful in her eyes. Mal froze, seeing it. She looked like how he'd felt, after...

"If I've broken the law," Etta said, her voice small and devastated, "I should do what she says."

"Oh, you've broken the law. But more than that, you're an active danger to everyone around you. I'm going to keep you warded until the queen can see you and we can decide what steps to take."

"She's part of the Fay clan, too, Lady Falcestershire. Le Fay should decide her fate."

"Is she?" The dowager countess smiled at Malcolm. "She's not on your official rolls. She hasn't taken the oaths. I could tell if she had."

The oaths were magical promises, sworn to the leader of the clan. They left an impression on the magic of the oath taker. "A formality. She's our blood."

Etta's head flopped to the side again, her earlier energy almost gone, but it was still clearly a denial. "No one's asked me to take an oath, Mal. And after what happened the other night, they would have, if they wanted me."

"Of course they want you—" A gag of air flew into his mouth.

"He's lying," Lady Falcestershire said. "The whole clan has been lying to you. Keeping secrets. Come with me, and the queen will tell you the truth, about who you are, and what role you have to play."

Etta stared at Lady Falcestershire, then at Malcolm. He

struggled against the gag, seeking to reconnect with her magic, but the pain was too intense and his magic was too weak.

"She's right about the secrets," Etta murmured. "Your mother as much as admitted there were things she knew that she wouldn't tell me. And I am a danger. If the queen can help...I'm sorry, Mal, but I have to go. I don't want to hurt anyone else."

Mal shook his head, but it did no good. Didn't she trust *him*? Didn't she believe *him*? Did his actions mean nothing? He'd risked everything, fought his fears and overcome them, and for what?

Lady Falcestershire released Etta's bonds, and Mal's gag. Etta collapsed, her eyes closed. Had she passed out? He would have gone to her, except that Lady Falcestershire flung up a hand again, warning him off. "Don't come any closer. She's just asleep. That was too much power for anyone to use at once, much less a half-trained chit. She'll be fine. If you promise to stay over there, I'll see to your arm."

He reluctantly nodded. She strode to him and grasped the break. "This will hurt. I'm sorry." She snapped the bone back into place, and he roared.

His vision whited out, bright spots covering everything, and agony tore into his brain as her fingers gripped the newly straightened forearm. When she released him, the brilliance changed to dark, and then he could see again. She drew a few quick threads of power around the injury, tying them off and marking symbols for healing over the net. "That should be stable by tomorrow, and healed in a few weeks, if you keep it immobilized. But it's going to hurt like hell. You should have left well enough alone."

The pain had shifted from a sharp spike to a deep throb, but he managed to force out words. His voice had gone gritty and rough from shouting, and it barely broke a whisper.

"Don't take her. There is more going on here than you know."

"There is more going on than *you* know, Lord Malcolm. This is Her Majesty's business, and none of yours. Now stay back. I'm going to open a portal."

Mal got out of the way. Portals were unreliable at the best of times, and took so much power that they were impractical for daily use. For her to cast one here and now, with the magical energy still so chaotic and fractured, showed that Lady Falcestershire was desperate to take Etta away from him.

The Queen's Sorceress drew down the few remaining tendrils of wild magic and formed the portal matrix. Mal lifted a trembling hand to his mouth when the spell actually came together, and didn't explode in all of their faces. Then she heaved Etta with another tendril of air, and both of them disappeared into the light.

Etta was gone, and Mal stood alone at the top of the cliff, staring at the spot where the woman he loved—the woman who had chosen to leave him—had vanished.

---

30 April 1895

Etta and I doused the fires in the cabin this evening and went down to the spring to build the Beltane bonfire. She kindled the blaze this year, calling up fire with the spell I taught her. It never worked for me, but she has no problems with it. We sat together all night, telling each other stories. I told her of the legends of our people, of the animal guides who still roamed the mountains, and the fair folk in Ireland and Scotland.

We re-lit the hearths from the bonfire before midnight. I suppose it is the first of May, not the last of April, but I'll let my date stand. It felt like a new beginning, tonight. Like it is time for something else. Etta is twenty years old, now, almost twenty-one, and no longer a child. We must speak of her future.

I'll leave that for the morning. I'm to bed.

-from the journal of Aileana Fay Cook

The portal opened in a roped-off courtyard in a seaside town. Etta had woken during the jolt of passage, though Amelia's spell still carried her. She managed a few little turns of her head, examining the white-washed brick of the courtyard walls and the open tunnel on the third side. Outside of the little passage lay a lane, a small seawall, and a harbor.

"Can you stand on your own?"

Etta's attention returned to the dowager countess. "I think so." Her voice croaked, as though she'd been able to scream out loud the sounds that had been trapped in her head on Skye.

Amelia released the spell, and offered her arm. Etta didn't want to take it, but had no choice. She was too weak to do anything else. When they touched, Etta could feel that holding the portal open had drained the other woman's magic considerably. But the ward she'd put around Etta was still firmly in place, and Etta didn't want to run. The voice in her head kept telling her to be wary, but she was so tired.

A clatter arose behind them, and a liveried footman appeared at Etta's side. She gave herself into his arms with relief. On his heels, a plump woman hurried out and bobbed a curtsey to Amelia.

"My apologies for the delay. We didn't know you were coming." She had a pleasant warm burr to her speech, but a different accent than the Fay clan.

"You couldn't have known, Mrs. Grant. I'll need a room and some clothes for my companion, and some tea for me while I wait. Then we'll take the carriage to Her Majesty."

"Of course, Lady Falcestershire." Mrs. Grant bobbed again, and waved a hand at the footman. He helped Etta across the courtyard and into the building. She staggered on the steps, so he picked her up and carried her to a small room. The walls were empty and white, the furniture Spartan, and the wide planks of the floor were rough against her still-bare feet.

He sat her on the bed, which proved to have a straw-ticked mattress. The similarity to her grass-stuffed one in the cabin almost made Etta weep. They were treating her like a servant, but for her, this was the closest she'd come in weeks to home.

She leaned listlessly against the bedpost while a maid brought a shapeless shift and a measuring tape, and two more footmen carried in a hipbath. She'd not allowed anyone to dress her since infancy, but she had to accept assistance getting undressed. Two maids had to hold her arms as she eased into the tub, or else she'd have fallen over. Everything ached, from the soles of her feet to the top of her head. She felt scraped and raw and like she'd been crying for hours, all hollowed out and sore.

Once she'd relaxed against the side of the bath, she luxuriated in the warmth that unknotted all her tense muscles. The sensation lasted for only a few moments before her eyes closed and she fell asleep.

The maids woke her again, handing her a cake of soap. She performed a perfunctory series of ablutions, and then settled back.

She couldn't find sleep again. Every time she closed her eyes, she saw the cliff, felt the raw power surging through her, saw Mal lying on the ground, his arm broken. He'd helped her channel the magic, but he'd been hurt. And what would happen next time, when he wasn't there?

Amelia was right. She was dangerous.

She sat in the tub until the water cooled. Misery and despair pooled in her heart, deep and vast as a sea, one she was far too exhausted to swim.

One of the women tugged on her arm, and she allowed

them to help her up, and dry her off, her body moving like an automaton, a clockwork construct holding only a simulacrum of life.

A dress appeared, procured by an older woman, along with a ready-made corset and combinations. Nothing fit well, and by the time the servants finished lacing the corset, tying on the bustle, and settling the gown over her petticoats, she could barely support the weight that fashionable society demanded. How she longed for her little cabin in the woods, and her comfortable trousers and boots.

Another maid arrived with a brush and pins and attacked her hair, wrestling the dark mass into a quasi-respectable arrangement.

Someone provided a looking glass, and the group at large deemed the effort presentable. Etta hoped the new garments would hide the emptiness, and the tremors that spasmed through her muscles.

Etta returned downstairs under her own power and met Amelia in a sitting room.

"Oh, much better," the lady said, setting down her tea and standing to take in the effect of the new dress and hair. "If we had more time, I would take you to a seamstress to adjust the fit, but Her Majesty will understand. She does not judge her subjects who do not have the means to dress in style."

Etta tried to ignore this unsubtle dig, and the others that followed as they rode in a well-appointed carriage down the streets of the town. One of the maids had told her it was called Stonehaven, and that the queen always passed through on her way to and from Balmoral Castle. When Amelia needed a hasty exit, she sometimes used their courtyard as a portal destination. The maid had whispered that she'd heard the sorceress had even had real gold laid under the cobbles for some arcane purpose.

Gold had many magical properties, but was not often

used because of the expense. As the Queen's Sorceress, though, Amelia could call on quite a few more resources than the average hedgewitch. If she'd used the gold to turn the courtyard into a part of her portal spell, that would make the spell more reliable and easier to cast. Too bad that wasn't a practical option for anyone else. It also explained why they had to take a carriage now. Such an inlay wouldn't work in reverse—it was a landing spot, not a casting spot.

The voice in her head, which had quieted while she'd been cleaned and dressed, murmured, *She's clever, but not enough.*

Etta shivered, and stared out the window. The shiver set off the headache that had eased in the bath, and the bumping of the carriage made it worse. She would have closed her eyes and tried to nap again, but the voice said, *Watch for a way back.*

Once out of the town, the landscape shifted abruptly to cultivated fields, and after an hour's drive, to hills and woods. At first, the dowager countess attempted to make conversation. She chattered about life in London and her travels, and told Etta again that she might call her Amelia, since they would be working together.

But Etta had no heart for conversation. She'd left her heart behind on Skye, and she would never recover it.

She'd made the wisest choice. Her actions had brought danger to the Fay family, and to Mal. There must be a way to control her magic that didn't threaten the people that she loved. But she ached with the separation. She'd finally found a home, and now she'd abandoned it.

The carriage finally came to a stop in a small drive before a large building of white stone that was caught somewhere between a manor house and a castle. It had a huge square tower on one end, and a more typical manor house on the other. It was the oddest place she'd ever seen. Emberlach, with its progression of styles and additions, had a feeling of cheery warmth and whimsy. Balmoral made Etta tremble.

Once inside the house, even more uneasiness settled within her. Amelia went off to speak with the queen, and left Etta alone in a cavernous foyer. It was a curious mix of opulence and wilderness. There were marble floors and statues and ornate carved moldings, but also deer heads mounted on the walls and arrangements of wildflowers similar to many she'd seen in cabins back in Fee's Holler.

Nothing in this place fit together, even the magic. She walked through a clear line of power, but then could feel nothing, as though someone had deliberately warded off sections of the castle and forced the energy to follow a proscribed path.

She'd come here half in fear of what she'd done, and half in hope that the queen and her sorceress could help, but every step told her that there would be no solace for her here.

The maid ushered her into a sitting room to await the queen's leisure, and Etta stared. Tartan swathed nearly every surface.

This house must be the royal idea of rusticating in the Scottish Highlands. She could not have come farther away from the one-room cabin on Roan Mountain than she was in this plaid-covered room. Great Mother, even the carpet was plaid!

A maid in—what else—tartan livery brought a tray of tea things to a table. She offered to pour, but Etta dismissed her and dropped gratefully onto the sofa. She made a cup with a touch of sugar, and sipped at it. The heat and the steam helped alleviate the worst of the headache that had returned while she jounced about in the carriage.

Nothing could ease the ache in her chest. Fee's Holler

wasn't home anymore, and this odd castle would never replace it.

She thought of the Fay School, with its students and the constant, comforting sensation of spells being cast. And of Emberlach, a working Highland estate where magic suffused every corner of the house and land. She'd belonged there. Why hadn't she demanded that Amelia allow her to go back? Why hadn't she thrown herself at Mal and begged him to take her home?

But home was not any of those places: not Roan Mountain, Glasgow, or Emberlach. Home was Malcolm Seward.

He'd tried to push her away, but he'd come when she needed him. He'd cast the spell for her, when she'd nearly lost herself inside the power on Skye. He'd faced his fears and they'd come through, together.

Why hadn't she faced hers, and turned to him?

Another maid arrived and interrupted her thoughts. "Her Majesty will see you now."

Etta took a deep breath, gripped her skirts, and walked out behind the woman. What she'd done at Fay House was still a mystery to her, and the queen would have to understand that she'd never intended to hurt anyone. She couldn't have known what kind of power had been waiting for her on Skye. No one could have. And if Mal hadn't come, things would have been much worse. She would argue for clemency for him. He shouldn't be punished because he'd followed her.

Great Mother. He'd followed her.

She stopped in the middle of the cavernous hallway, and the maid looked back at her with surprise. "Miss?"

Etta had made a mistake. She should not have agreed to go with Amelia, no matter that she'd claimed she had the right. Mal had come for her. He'd tried to tell her something, there at the end, and she should have listened.

But it was too late now. She was here, and the queen waited.

Etta entered an even larger drawing room, clenching her skirts in her fists to keep her hands steady. More plaid covered the floor and the drapes, clashing with the floral wallpaper and ornate statuary. Etta wasn't sure where to look—the room was so busy with riotous patterns.

Finally her gaze settled on a large woman, sitting on a tartan settee. She had a round, pale face with stern features, and wore unrelieved black except for a plain white veil on her head. She was the only thing in the room without decoration. Amelia's dress had profusions of lace, embroidery, and stripes on the colorful fabric.

Amelia presented her to the queen, who bade her be seated once she'd made her curtsey. Etta was never more thankful for a corset —even an ill-fitted corset—than now, as it forced her posture to remain upright and correct. She might otherwise have forgotten and slouched.

"We have heard many things about you, Miss Cook," the queen said. "What interests Us most is that you seem to be descended entirely in the female line from Lilias Fay."

Etta nodded, and stammered, "Y-yes, Your Majesty." What did her family history have to do with the magic she'd wrought on Skye?

"Interesting." The queen folded her hands. "Do the other members of Clan Fay know of your lineage?"

"I haven't hidden it, Your Majesty." Was she supposed to say Your Majesty every time?

The queen gestured to Amelia, who placed a piece of paper into her hands. "We have here a copy of the Letters Patent, granting the title Duchess of Fay to Lilias Fay by Our uncle, who was then the Prince Regent, on behalf of Our grandfather King George." She turned the document so that

Etta could see the calligraphic letters, although they were too far away to read.

The queen flipped the page back and scanned it with a finger. "Here is the relevant passage: 'And for Us Our heirs and successors do appoint give and grant unto her the said name state degree style dignity title and honour of Duchess of Fay to have and to hold the said name state degree style dignity title and honour of Duchess of unto her and the heirs female of her body lawfully begotten and to be begotten.'"

The Sovereign looked up from the page, and her cold gaze pierced Etta. The weight of all of her titles pressed behind that stare, and Etta remembered that she was considered an Empress, not only a queen.

"You are the heir female of her body." The queen slid the paper aside, revealing another, this one written in a far less-legible script on a typed page. There were several other sheets beneath. "These documents are proof that you lawfully begotten."

"Does 'lawfully begotten,' mean that my parents were married?"

"Yes," Amelia said. "Not only yours, but your mother's and her mother's, too. These are marriage licenses, sworn and witnessed, proving that everyone in your line is legitimate."

The queen placed the Letters Patent and the licenses on the low table in front of her, where Etta could now see them.

Etta stared at the pages. The letters refused to coalesce into words. She could not produce meaning from the curlicued script, or the badly-aligned typeset. Her magic shook and trembled, blurring her vision. The deep and complex aroma of a plowed field after a summer storm surrounded her, mixed with the bitter tang of lightning. "I don't understand," she said, and her voice was like the paper, dry and dusty.

"The Fay clan has been keeping secrets from you since

you first set foot in England," the monarch said. "We had Our suspicions, so We had Our sorceress investigate you. But the Fay family has known all along. You are the Duchess of Fay."

Etta's gaze leapt from the letter to the queen's face. "Excuse me if this is impertinent, Your Majesty, but what exactly does that mean?"

The queen settled back in her chair. Had Etta offended the monarch? But Her Majesty answered the question. "The Duchy of Fay has always been something of a...contentious position. My uncle, may the gods give his soul peace, was not much interested in governance." Her use of the singular 'my' was a hint that she spoke, not as queen, but as a woman. As Victoria.

"His Grace, the Duke of Wellington, required that Lilias Fey receive a title for her actions in the campaign against Bonaparte, particularly at Waterloo. More, he insisted that the title be equal to his own, and not a lifetime honor. Lilias demanded that the Letters Patent be written in the style of some of the Irish and Scottish titles, where it is not patrilineal primogeniture but matrilineal primogeniture that prevails. The Prince Regent acquiesced to their demands. The Duchy of Fay is the only title in the Peerage of the United Kingdom that passes in this manner, and so We felt a woman's hand was needed." Now she was the sovereign, using the royal We.

"When the third duchess died in 1887, attempts were made by the Committee of Privileges to locate any surviving children of Marianne Fay O'Flynn."

The queen paused here, and her gaze shifted from Etta to Amelia. The dowager countess resumed the narrative. "The committee spoke to your family, so we have records of those conversations. Le Fay and the Marchioness of Hazelby were consulted. At the time, only Lady Hazelby was aware of your existence."

"She wrote to my mother. I know because Ma mentioned it in her journal." She tapped her fingers against her thigh. "Why did no one come for me? It can't have been that hard to track down Marianne, if you were able to find all of these documents." She picked up the stack. "Great-Gran was an outspoken abolitionist, and a proponent of medical magic. I know she was in the papers constantly, before and after the War."

Etta stopped herself, as something horrible occurred to her. "Unless you did find her, and her children. Gran had just died in 1887, and she was a skip. Ma was a wild talent." Etta's hands trembled, and the letters rustled in her grasp. "You knew, but you didn't want the Duchess of Fay to be more Choctaw medicine woman than European witch."

"We knew," the queen admitted. "And yes, We…neglected to persist in the search, once Our agents located your mother. It was clear that she had no wish to leave America, and would not choose to become a duchess."

"And now that I'm here?" She tossed the papers onto the table. "What do you expect of me?"

"You are not your mother, Duchess." There was the slightest emphasis on the title, and Etta remembered that she wasn't supposed to address the queen as 'you.' But spitting out 'your majesty' instead was a little much to ask at the moment. "Lady Falcestershire tells Us you are well-suited to English magic. We require that you be a model to Our people of an accomplished—and proper—English witch. Too many of England's young witches and mages follow Our son and his extravagances, and the people are not forgiving of such excesses. We must curb his destructive impulses."

"So you want me to be some kind of figurehead for demure, inoffensive magic? I suppose that's why Amelia kept asking me about the Irish. You believe if you can parade me around as Duchess of Fay, the rabble will be reassured that not every mage follows your son's lead, and the Irish will be appeased to have a real witch in Parliament." Etta sat forward, ignoring the creaking of her corset as it protested the movement. "What if I turn out to be a powerful battle mage, like my great-great-grandmother?"

"You have already proven yourself a danger around strong magic," Amelia said. "What happened at Skye might happen again. You must learn control. I can teach you."

Etta flinched at the reminder, but there was something wrong about all of this. "Do you mean control, or suppression? Because I haven't seen you do much magic since we met. Does the Queen's Sorceress have to vow only to do necessary spells?"

Amelia's shoulders and upper body shifted backward and her posture stiffened. Her doll's face turned petulant. "We suppress excess magic only to maintain a consistent, non-threatening presence. It does not do to remind the lower classes that magic can be used to subjugate and enthrall them."

"No, you save that for the colonies. I've read the newspapers." Etta stood. The trembling inside of her ceased, turning to a core of molten heat. She should never have come here. "I'll not be Your Majesty's pawn." Her voice was soft, but steady as the Scottish mountains. "I don't need to be a duchess. You can take that away from me if you like. But you can't keep me from being trained, or from following my own heart and head, and making my own decisions."

The queen's gaze remained locked with hers for a long time. Etta would not back down. She had been born in a country that recognized no sovereign, whose people refused to bend a knee to anyone. No title alone could cow her. Of course, this woman was much more than a title, and her strength of will and personality were impressive. But so were Etta's.

Her heart pounded in her ears, each beat underscoring her determination. She set her jaw and lifted her chin, squaring her shoulders at the queen. No one in the world was as stubborn as a Cook, Ma used to say.

Perhaps no one was as stubborn, but Amelia was wilier. Etta did not see the spell coming, and it slammed into her, knocking her onto the sofa.

"If you will not submit, you must be contained," the queen said, and relaxed into her seat as Amelia prowled forward.

Etta opened her Sight and grappled with the lines of force in the room. She had no idea what she was doing and her threads dragged and pulled, sluggish and slow, as though she were trying to cast the spell deep underwater.

Inside Etta's mind, a woman's voice shouted, *Use your internal resources! The room is warded so only she can make use of the magic in here.*

Etta took a deep breath, and grasped the core of her magic. It pulsed at her mental touch, and she almost screamed in shock. It barely resembled what had been at her core the night of the blood-unity spell. She had noticed a few changes after making love to Mal, but whatever had happened on Skye had infused her with power and strength.

Mal. Would he help her, if she reached out to him? Or would he turn her away, as she had turned away from him?

Only one way to learn the answer. She sent her magic out, piercing through the ward, across the miles, to the other half of her heart.

He responded.

As it had from the first, his magic meshed with hers, even across a wild distance. Except that he wasn't nearly as far away as he should be. Or in the right direction.

No time for questions. Something tried to break through their bond, and the connection began to waver.

I need your help! His power surged from wherever he was,

and she grasped it, hard. She would not allow Amelia to cut her off from him. But she didn't know what else to do.

I'm here. What's going on?

I need that battle magic you told me about. Amelia was crafting something, and it looked wicked, with jagged edges that would tear through Etta's magic like thorns.

Are we attacking the queen? Mal's mental voice should have felt shocked, but instead there was almost glee.

Not the queen. Lady Falcestershire. And I don't want to hurt her. I just want to get out of this room.

I have to take control. He was still angry with her, and tired, and in pain. His own magical resources were nearly spent. She tried to make him feel her regret, her desire to go back to Skye and make a very different choice.

Idiot. I know. Give me your hands.

She surrendered.

Her hands began to move without her conscious direction, pulling threads of power from her core and forming them into distinct webs. She threw the webs at Amelia, who had been weaving a second spell that looked more like a ward or binding.

Mal's spells shredded the still unformed ward and struck Amelia full in the face. She staggered back, and the queen cried out.

"I thought you said she wouldn't be able to do magic!"

Amelia shook her hand and swiped at her face, as though she could remove the tendrils of magic that had adhered over her skin. She managed to say, "She can't. I don't know how she's doing this—" before the spell covered her mouth.

Etta was not about to reveal Mal's assistance, so she merely backed away from the queen and Amelia. "I don't want to hurt anyone. Let me go."

"You only hurt yourself if you leave," the queen said. She had not stood, but she no longer looked at ease. "You are a danger to Our people in your current state. We are within Our rights to detain you."

No, she isn't. That wasn't Mal's voice, but the woman's again. *Swear allegiance to Clan Fay right now, and she will have to let you go. Clan law still rules magic in Scotland.*

Lilias is right. That was Mal. Did he truly mean Lilias? The original duchess? *Yes, that Lilias. But she's right. If you're a member of the clan, they can't hold you.*

He'd offered this, when they were on Skye, and she'd been too wrapped up in her own despair to recognize it for the precious gift it was. And Lilias hadn't said a word then. *You wanted to see the queen, didn't you? You've been dead ten years and there's something you needed to know. What is it?*

The voice of the geas didn't respond, and Mal said, *Now isn't the time. Swear the oath, Etta.*

She stared at the two women on the opposite settee. *They won't let me walk away.*

Amelia wouldn't, Mal agreed, *but without legal recourse, and with the threat of violence, I think Her Majesty will choose to fight another day.*

Her hands were moving again, and she wasn't sure if it was Mal or, incredibly, her long-dead great-great-grandmother who guided the spell. But this one wasn't meant to attack. It settled over her as she spoke the words: "I pledge my allegiance to the Clan Fay, and bind myself to serve its interests for all of my days."

"No!" Amelia had managed to free herself from Mal's spell, and she now flung another jet of power at Etta. Etta's arms moved in an instinctive gesture, and she had no idea if it was her instinct, Mal's, or Lilias's. A wall of magic sprang between her body and the attack.

"Let me go," she said again. "You cannot hold me. I am a member of the Fay clan, and subject to their rules and laws. Only Le Fay can decide what to do with me now."

Amelia prepared another spell, but the queen held up a single, imperious hand. The trembling black ruffle in her cuffs betrayed only the slightest hint of emotion.

Her gaze locked with Etta's, and once again it was a struggle between Queen and Duchess. Then, to Etta's surprise, the monarch smiled. It was not a happy smile. No, this was the smile of a hunter who has discovered worthy prey. "So be it."

Etta released the barrier spell, and it snapped back into her with the force of a lash. She wanted to let go, to collapse, to accept the queen's defeat and relax, but the power still riding her from Skye did not allow her to retreat. So she spoke again. "You'll let me go?"

"I will. When you have completed your training, I will send for you, and we will speak again."

Etta flinched at the queen's use of the singular pronoun. Should feel relieved, or even more alarmed? For now, she only wanted to escape this castle and find Mal.

She strode out of the room and into a hallway. A maid found her after a half-dozen paces and showed her to the front hall. The carriage was gone, so she would have to walk.

Where are you? she asked Mal.

In Stonehaven. I re-cast Lady Falcestershire's portal and ended up in a courtyard by the harbor. But it took me forever, and you were already gone.

Do you think you could cast another to Balmoral?

No. I don't know enough about portal spells. I only copied the dowager countess's, and I still almost got it wrong.

He might not know, but I do. Lilias again.

How are you alive in my head? Etta asked.

It's a geas, Mal answered. *She isn't truly there. It's the part of Lilias that cast the spell on you. I have no idea how she did it, but a geas has to have a consciousness directing it. She managed to split hers enough to maintain the geas even after she died, which is supposed to be impossible.*

It is not impossible. Merely difficult. Portals, however, are not difficult. At least, they will not be for you. I will show you.

Etta's fingers began to move again. *Stop that. I want to cast my own spells, thank you very much.*

You are casting it yourself. Think of this as a much closer variety of shadowcasting.

Her hands continued shaping a spell, drawing from the wind and sunlight and the warm life force of millions of tiny organisms all around her in the soil.

The threads were far more intricate than any she'd cast before. Even the spell on Skye, with Malcolm, had been cast using massive threads, each one as thick as her wrist or larger. The portal spell—while powerful by most standards—was more delicate and subtle.

Her mouth formed words, she gave them voice, and the portal opened.

She stepped through to Stonehaven.

The portal closed with a crack and Etta stumbled onto the cobblestones underlain with gold. Mal threw himself at her, and before she could say a word, he sealed his lips against hers.

Don't ever leave me again.

Don't ever push me away.

Their thoughts crossed, and they held each other more tightly.

Then—as one—a thought arose, full of heat and light and promises.

I love you.

-a page is torn out-

? May 1895

I dreamed of the North again last night. This fever came so sudden, and will not let me go.

I fear that death is stalking me.

? May 1895

Etta, my love, when you read this, I will be gone. This is my first lucid moment since Beltane, but I will not wake you. You look exhausted from taking care of me.

There is so much I never told you, about our family, about the past. I should have done so long ago, but I was selfish. I wanted you with me, and safe. Your great-gran never wavered in her conviction that we were better off with an ocean between us and the rest of the clan. But I have not been a good teacher to you, and perhaps not a good mother, either. You are old enough to have finished your training. I am so sorry that I have held you back from what you might have become. It is time for you to go to them, and to learn all that they can teach you.

Please forgive me, love. I shall miss you, but I will not linger. I long to see your Papa again. He is calling me, from across the veil. I must answer.

My love for you is eternal, but my body is not. Good-bye, my darling girl.

-from the journal of Aileana Fay Cook

Mal convinced Etta to stay in Stonehaven for the night. They both required rest, and he complained that he needed to sleep with his arms around her—even if one of those arms was now wrapped in a brace—and not propped in a railcar on their way back to Emberlach.

He told the proprietor at the inn that they were married, and Etta teased—once they were alone in their room—that if they did marry, he would become a duke by marriage.

"Don't even say it." He buried his face in her neck, and nipped at the sensitive spot at the edge of her jaw. Then he drew back, his blue eyes full of mirth. "Though I suppose I should have guessed it would be you, even before my mother told me."

"Your mother told you?" Etta pushed him away, and glowered at him.

"Yes, the morning after you left. She and Muireall had decided to train you, and were going to break the news to you then. But I should have figured it out before that."

"How?"

"Because Beatrice was Duchess after my great-grandma Horatia." Mal put both hands around her head and leaned to nuzzle her nose with his. "If the title was going to pass normally, my grandfather Silas should have been the next Duke. But he wasn't. He took his father's title, Earl of Clary." He tried to kiss her, but she turned her mouth aside, and his lips met her cheek. He pretended to bite her.

"It's matrilineal," Etta said, poking him in the chest for the pretense. "Lilias insisted." There was a little murmur in Etta's mind at the use of the name, but she clamped down on the geas, the way Mal had shown her once she arrived. He'd explained what it was, and why Lilias had cast it. But neither of them knew what to do about it now, or why it seemed to have agendas of its own. She'd asked it again about why it let her go to the queen rather than having her swear her oath to the clan on Skye, but although Etta was certain she had the right of it, the geas remained stubbornly silent. Perhaps now it had what it wanted—Etta had taken up her place as duchess, and was in love. She and Mal would eventually have children, and the title would pass on. She pressed a little harder, and the murmuring ceased. She wouldn't allow a spell to ruin this night with him.

"The title can only pass mother-to-daughter." She let the implication of that, and her willingness to contemplate a future wherein she might have a child—when she would have *his* child—fill her voice. Their gazes met, and they stood for a moment, Mal's fingers twined in her hair, their breath mingling in the tiny space between their bodies.

"Then I suppose we'd better have lots of daughters." One side of his mouth quirked in her favorite of his grins.

Etta put her hands on his chest, and he wrapped his arms around her. She relaxed into his embrace. "You don't mind, then?"

"That I'd be marrying a Duchess? I admit, I'd not have

asked for it. I'm still terrified that my brother won't have any boys and I'll become Marquess of Hazelby. But the title of Duchess is invested in you, so, no. I don't mind."

She'd pulled her hair down from the arrangement made by Amelia's servants, and Mal stroked his fingers through the strands that fell down her back.

"So, must one of us formally ask, or do we simply accept that we belong together?" She ran a finger over his breastbone, and down to his belly.

"We accept." He captured the finger, and brought it to his lips.

Etta raised on tiptoe to replace her finger with her mouth. Then she relaxed into his embrace. "I love you, Cuthbert Malcolm Elliott Seward. I will marry you, and be your wife, and carry our children. Though I'd like to wait until my training is finished for that last part." She kissed him again. This time, the kiss was a promise.

He broke away, at last, to say, "I love you, too, you know. I can wait as long as you'd like for children. I want no one else to wife but you, Henrietta Mairi Cook."

Etta groaned. "How did you know my full name?"

"Mother found a letter in her great-aunt Beatrice's things. It was from your mother, written about the same time you were born. Beatrice wrote a note on the back, saying that she'd given the letter to the duchess, and it had been returned on her death. Lilias wrote something on it, too. You should see it."

"I'd like to, when we get back. There is so much I need to learn."

"Yes, there is. And there's so much I want to teach you." He seized her hand again, kissing each fingertip in turn. "My duchess. I'll have the banns read in the village when we return."

Etta gasped as he laved her palm with his tongue. Then she asked, "What are banns?"

A laugh erupted up from his belly. He leaned down, captured her lovely mouth with his, and propelled her back toward the bed.

~

"THAT GIRL IS GOING TO BE TROUBLE," AMELIA SAID, PRESSING a cold cloth to her forehead where the spell had hit, leaving a bruise.

"Yes, but I think she is going to prove more trouble for Clan Fay than for me." The queen sat at her writing desk, penning a letter. She wrote another line, then paused. "Tell me again about the power you felt on Skye."

"It was enormous. I don't know how the old witch did it." A reluctant admiration filled Amelia. She'd clashed with Lilias on a number of occasions during her early days out in Society, and the duchess had been formidable. "She's either got some Power Wells in the family vault that are bigger than anything short of the Royal Armory, or she managed to manipulate the leylines in the area to fill in a secret pocket on their property."

The queen's pen paused mid-stroke. "Which do you think it is?"

Amelia considered the question a moment, spreading the cloth so that it covered both aching temples. She closed her eyes and answered. "It is more likely the Wells. Leyline manipulation is tricky, and Lilias would have needed help. Once more than one person knows a secret, it isn't a secret anymore." She opened her eyes again and found the queen looking at her. "After fighting Napoleon, Lilias knew the value of secrets better than anyone."

"Do you believe she crafted them herself, or found them?" Her Majesty's attention returned to the letter.

"I couldn't speculate." Amelia opened the cloth and draped it over most of her face, leaving only her mouth free. "She was a canny witch, and she could have divined how to make them. But she also traveled, and the Continent was riven by chaos for much of the time she was there. She could have found the missing Wells from the Chanteur Treasury, lost during the French Revolution, or some private collection heretofore unknown."

"Go back to Skye and find out for sure. And if they have Wells, they must be retrieved."

Amelia frowned, hiding the expression with the now tepid cloth. "Fay House is well protected. It will take time."

"We have time. The chit won't be trained in a day."

No point in arguing with the queen. Her Majesty did not accept such frivolous concepts as practical restrictions or reality. Amelia acquiesced, placed the cloth on a platter, and begged to take her leave. Once it was granted, she stalked out to the big garden behind the house. There, with the Scottish sky above her, she flung her magical senses into a wide arc, drawing energy back into herself. She would need all of her wits and all of her strength to do as she'd been ordered.

Amelia turned to face almost due west—toward Skye—and began to plan.

MAL WOKE TO THE BEST FEELING HE'D EVER HAD. ETTA WAS still in his arms. One of those arms still ached like fury and the other was numb from his lover's weighty skull, but he couldn't stop the grin that stretched across his face.

She'd agreed to marry him, and he'd done several spells—

some of them in conjunction with Etta—and no one had been harmed.

Nothing could possibly dampen his spirits today.

He carefully extricated his deadened limb and climbed out of bed. He pulled the covers around Etta and went to the washstand to clean his teeth and scrub up a bit. The only thing he missed about London was the hot water pipes that made bathing an easy and solitary affair. Even in good Scottish inns, he still had to call for maids and footmen to bring hot water and a tub.

A rustle of bedclothes heralded Etta's awakening. He turned to watch her. She grumbled and stretched, her dark hair half in her face. He took a step toward her with some thought of brushing it back, but she flopped back against the pillow and did the job herself.

"What time is it?" Her normally charming accent sounded even sharper and higher this morning.

"Half six. You're a lovely sight when you wake." He made his tone bright and cheery, and was rewarded with a pillow flung in his direction. It didn't go the distance, flopping at the foot of the bed, but he decided that was worth a return bit of affection, and crawled over the bedsheets to her, careful not to put his full weight on the broken arm.

"Yesterday, I fell under a geas crafted by my many-years-dead great-grandmother and had to channel a massive amount of power into a leyline spell. Then I fought the Queen's Sorceress and managed to best Queen Victoria. After that, I engaged in some vigorous sexual calisthenics with the man I love. I'm allowed to be a bit grouchy this morning."

"Of course, my dearest love." He pulled her arms away from her face and kissed her forehead. "Would you like me to ring for a breakfast tray, or shall we go down to the common room?"

Etta's expression turned from near-mirth to near-horror. "Make a servant bring me food because I'm tired? I don't think so." She scrambled up, and some of Mal's humor faded with the motion.

"I wasn't trying to chastise you."

"I know." She rooted around in the pile of her clothing on the floor, and Mal couldn't help admiring the sight of her ass, lovely and round and pointed right at him. "It's only that I don't like others doing for me when I am capable of taking care of myself."

He slid off the bed and strode over to her, grasping her hips and pressing the part of his anatomy that most appreciated the view against the fascinating curve. She straightened, and leaned into him. The warm skin of her back pressed against his chest, and he rested his chin on the top of her head.

"Sometimes it's nice to have someone else take care of… certain things." He wrapped his arms around her body. With the hand of the broken arm, he stroked a breast, its tip already hard and peaked with the chilled air, and with the other, he cupped her mound. His fingers pressed through her mat of dark curls and found her plump, warm flesh.

"Mmm…I'll not disagree with that." She rubbed her lovely arse against him, and he twirled them until she faced the bed. He leaned her over, and she went willingly, grabbing the mattress to steady her. It was the perfect height for him to fit himself into her. He teased her a little, first, stroking her clitoris and nipples, and then slid a finger into her cunny. It was tight, and wet, and he bit the back of her neck to stifle his groan. He positioned his cock against her wet folds and thrust into her. She closed her muscles around him in a tight grasp, and demanded, "keep touching me," as she pushed back against him.

She didn't need to ask. He stroked the hood of her clit,

slow at first, matching every thrust, and then faster, until she was panting and moaning and finally screamed into the coverlet. Her cunny spasmed and clutched at his shaft, and it took only a few more pumps of his hips until he emptied himself inside her.

They lay like that, sated, for a few minutes, before she shifted her hips and his soft, wet cock slipped out of her. She wriggled around in his arms and pressed a brief kiss on his mouth. Then she pulled away. "Now I should wash, use the water closet, and get dressed. I want to get something to eat before we go to the train station. It's time to return to Emberlach and start my training."

Mal tugged her back into his arms—he wasn't finished with her yet—and sealed his lips to hers. He slid his tongue into her mouth and stroked her until she moaned with pleasure. Then he broke away and grinned. "Let's go."

A FEW DAYS' TRAVEL LATER, MAL FOLLOWED VIOLA TO THE BIG sitting room in the public wing at Emberlach, where she'd gathered the members of the clan. Viola carried baby Adaira on her shoulder. Mother was seated at the escritoire, writing. Sorcha read in a chair by the big window. Muireall had the clan's Book of Shadows and Light open on her lap. Ian stood by the door, dressed in work clothes and smelling of animals. He must have come straight from the barn, though his face and hands were clean. He held baby Andrew in the crook of his arm.

The extended family was there, too—all of the cousins and uncles, and even those joined to the clan by marriage vows rather than blood.

Mal gestured behind him, and Etta came to stand in the doorway. She looked so beautiful, even travel-rumpled and cross from being stuck in a little box on wheels for days. He held out his hand and she stepped forward and linked her fingers with his.

"Members of Clan Fay, may I present Her Grace, Lady Henrietta Mairi Cook Fay, the Duchess of Fay."

Silence reigned for a moment, stealing their collective voices. Then everyone spoke at once. In the tumult, Mal pulled Etta against his side. He loved that he could stand together with her like this, and no longer had to fear his mother or anyone else would try to keep them apart.

"Etta."

They both turned at his mother's voice. Everyone else had quieted, and she stood alone in the center of the room. It was the first time that Mother had addressed Etta informally. And she'd done so after learning that Etta was now her social superior, which usually made Mother's formality increase exponentially. Something had changed in her, the night of the twins' birth.

Then she came to them, and wrapped her arms around them both. Etta wriggled away from Mal, and burrowed into the welcoming embrace.

"The queen acknowledged you, then?" his mother asked.

Etta's voice was muffled. "Yes." She broke away a little. "And you knew! This whole time, you knew."

"I knew that your mother had claimed you were a matrilineal descendent, and the blood-unity spell proved that was true. So, if you were legitimate, and so was your mother, the title was yours. But, though I asked, Her Majesty never deigned to inform me of the results of the committee for privileges findings. So I hesitated to tell you. But we were going to share everything, the morning after the twins were born."

"I'm legitimate. Her Majesty has all of the documentation and everything."

"Good." His mother lifted her hand and stroked a strand of hair away from Etta's face. "Do you remember what I told you, before, about my reasons?"

"You told me nothing, except that they were good ones." Her lips turned down in a little frown of accusation.

"Some of them are still true. I'm afraid that you will either be the making or the breaking of our clan, Etta. But I see now that I must help you if we are to succeed."

"At stopping the drain on English magic?" Etta asked.

"There's plenty of time to take on the family windmill, my dear," Muireall said from behind Mal's shoulder. "Let's get you trained up a bit, first."

Then Viola and Ian were there, asking questions about the journey and the queen, and it seemed like hours before Mal could pull Etta away.

He sent a maid ahead to ready a bath, and made another mental note to speak to his mother about installing a water heater and a bathing chamber or two in the family wing. As it was, he had to wait for the tub and water to be brought in. But eventually everything was in place, the servants were gone, and he finally had Etta to himself.

ETTA WAS UNACCOUNTABLY NERVOUS. IT HAD ONLY BEEN A week since they'd made love in his bed in the adjoining room. They'd explored every inch of each other's flesh, and found intense pleasure in their discoveries.

But that was before she was a duchess, and before they'd agreed to marry.

Their two couplings in Stonehaven had been purely physical, with both of their magical energies drained. Now, they were recovered, and she couldn't hide behind shock or desperation.

Her hands shook as she tried to open the buttons on her dress.

Mal's fingers engulfed hers. "I'll see to that." He deftly unbuttoned and unhooked and unlaced until she was clad only in her chemise. But still, she trembled.

"What's wrong, love?"

"I know you said you didn't mind, but I think—maybe—that *I* mind."

"Mind what? Being a duchess?"

She couldn't answer in words, so she leaned back against him and nodded.

"Eventually you're going to be Le Fay, too, you know."

"I've a long way to go before I match Muireall, and that will be a title I earn. It won't be saddled on me because of my birth, like a filly you're hoping will be a champion because her grand-dame won the Triple Crown."

"You'd have to earn that, too, if you were a horse. But I know what you mean. Trust me when I say that the title doesn't have to define who you are."

"You don't want to be a marquess."

"I don't want to have my father's responsibilities. But I'm a creature of fire and water, and you're good, solid earth." He nuzzled her neck. "That's the other thing about titles. They are what you make of them. You would never want to be the kind of peer who spends to excess, bankrupting his estate and beggaring his tenants. You'll be a good steward of the Fay properties. Plus, Lilias had a seat in Parliament. Great-Grandmother Horatia and Great-Aunt Beatrice never took up their seats, but Lilias used to rain fire on the opposition with her speeches."

He ran his hands over her as he spoke, calming her spirit and arousing her flesh. All of those things sounded…solid. Practical. Real. The opposite of fashionable. The opposite of illusory. And that is what she feared about becoming a

Duchess. That the title would be a glittering façade with nothing inside.

"The title doesn't have to be empty," Mal murmured. He'd sunk into her with his magic, and her thoughts were clear to them both. "It can be like your magic, essential to who you are. You can be Etta Mae, and the Duchess of Fay, and my wife, and a damn good witch, and some day mother to our children. It won't be a sham, if you make it real."

She clung to his reassurance like a hand holding her tight as she dangled over a cliff. Beneath her, beyond her, was the unknown. A new life, as her mother had told her on Beltane. That felt like ages ago, instead of months.

But with this man beside her, and with her new family at her back, perhaps she would not fall. Perhaps she would fly.

Etta twisted in Mal's arms and took his mouth with hers. His tongue swept into her mouth, and she stroked hers along it. His hard cock nudged her belly when she pressed her body against him. She pulled away a little and tugged at his trousers.

He took the hint, and in moments, they were naked together. She grabbed the toweling beside the bath and spread it out on the floor. Then she pulled Mal down and straddled him. She was wet for him already, and gasped as she took him into her body.

How she'd needed this, how she'd needed him.

"I love you." She leaned forward and kissed him, then settled back to ride.

"I love you." His words came out on a moan, and she laughed, then gasped as she slid down his length and his hip pressed against her sensitive flesh. She had wanted slow, languorous lovemaking, but as her breath caught, she moved faster, driving them both higher. Mal slid his thumb over her clitoris, stroking it in counterpoint to his body moving inside of her.

Heat and light shot through her from the place where they joined, from each touch of his hand, rising and cresting and dragging her up until she shattered, her body trembling and shuddering over him.

He took her hips in his hands then, holding her still as he thrust up into her, hard and fast, until he groaned and shuddered with his own release.

She collapsed against his chest.

A small eternity later, Mal stroked her hair. "We'd better use that bath before it gets cold, Duchess."

She laughed. "As you wish, Lord Cuthbert."

"Gods, woman, pax. Let's both agree to never speak that name again." But he chuckled.

The tub was—just barely—big enough for two.

EPILOGUE

1 May 1895

I dreamed of Scotland. There was a woman in my dream, with flaming hair, flashing hazel eyes, and skin that would have been milk-pale if not for a profusion of freckles. She sat on the top of a mountain, looking down toward the sea. Around her skirts was a spell-ring, full of symbols made of salt. She looked surprised to see me. Her Scotch accent was thick. I wonder how long it took my father's people to lose theirs, here in America?

She asked me who I was, and I answered her.

"Och. You're one of mine," she said.

"Yours?"

"I can feel it, in your blood. Can't you?"
And then I could. And I knew who she was. "You're Lilias, aren't you?"

"I am. What path will I take, I wonder, that leads to you, daughter-of-my-blood?"

"What do you mean by that?"

"No offense meant, my dear. But it's clear that you're from the colonies. Forgive me, the new America. You've the look of a Mohawk scout who came back to Scotland with my uncle Angus after the rebellion."

"I'm Choctaw," I answered. "But what do you mean, 'will I take?' You're dead."

She laughed. "Not yet, dear one. I'm younger than you are. I tried this spell to contact an ancestor, but it appears I've conjured a descendant instead."

"I'm descended from your youngest daughter."

"Don't tell me any more, please. I don't wish to know about my future. I wanted to know about my past. Or perhaps, our past. There's something...wrong with magic in Britain. I don't know what it is, and I was hoping a perspective from history would help."

"What do you mean, wrong?" Gran always said she had good reasons to leave. Maybe keeping Etta away wasn't such a bad choice after all.

"Magic is fading. Something is draining magic from these shores, and I don't know what it is."

"I'm afraid I can't help you. I've never been to Scotland, except in dreams."

"Perhaps you can assure that, in your time, someone is still trying to fix the problem." Those hazel eyes pierced through me. In dreams, you have no flesh, and your soul is laid bare. She rose, never leaving the circle of salt, and held out her hands. She cast the most elaborate spell net I have ever seen, so intricate and fine I could not even tell where some parts ended and others began. "Forgive me, daughter of my line. I lay this geas upon you, and your heirs. Find out what is stealing magic from the British Isles. And, if you can, steal it back."

-from the journal of Aileana Fay Cook, page torn out and slipped into the lining

Etta fingered the letters her mother had sent to the Fays over the years, laid out on the desk in the study of her and Mal's apartments in the Fay School of Magic in Glasgow. Cecily had wanted them to rent a townhouse, or stay with her outside the city in another of the family properties, but Etta liked being close to her classes and the other students. She also liked the austerity of the little apartment. It was furnished plainly, but serviceably, and had a bedroom, a study, and an all-purpose room that doubled as dining area and sitting room. They had to share the water closet and bathing chambers with Muireall and her family, and had to eat on the schedule determined by the school's cook, but had more privacy than in the student dorms.

Compared to both her tiny cabin growing up and the grandeur of the Seward houses, their little rooms were heaven.

Nearly all of the letters in front of Etta had been addressed to Beatrice, the third Duchess of Fay. A single missive—the last—had been addressed to Cecily. Etta recognized some of the contents from events her mother had written about in her journals.

But as lovely as it was to see her mother's familiar handwriting, and to drink in her mother's words, it was the notes Lilias had written on the letters that interested Etta most.

Sorcha had given Etta all of Lilias's correspondence and papers, including her entire ninety-year series of journals. The volumes were spelled to open only for the Duchess of Fay. Or perhaps they would have opened for any direct female descendant, as Etta couldn't imagine how a spell would be able to tell that she'd been officially invested with the title not long after her confrontation with the queen. She would still be required to go down to London and be presented at court next Season, but that was six months away and she had much training—and reading—to do in the meantime.

Lilias had been a faithful diarist. She wrote almost every day, even during the Napoleonic campaigns in Spain, Portugal, and France. The note written on the back of Aileana's first letter to Beatrice, informing her that her sister Marianne had died, included a reference to one of the earlier journal entries.

This one was dated 1 May, 1802. It was no coincidence that what Lilias described—conjuring a descendant from America, and laying a geas on her—was on the same day the terrible fever had descended on Etta's mother, ninety-three years later. Had Lilias's spell been the cause of her mother's death? It was possible. Binding wild talents with more "civilized" magic always had unexpected consequences. And Lilias could not have known that her great-granddaughter's magic was so alien to her own.

Etta shuddered and thrust both the letter and the journal down.

She pushed her chair away from the desk and went to find her husband.

Mal was ensconced in his favorite chair by the fire in the sitting room, reading letters from the new estate manager he'd hired to oversee his land in his absence. The armchair was worn with age and use, and some of the wool stuffing peeked out in places. But it was large, and sturdy, and comfortable for a variety of activities.

He put down his letters when Etta entered, and she hiked up her skirts and sat on him, straddling his legs and wrapping her arms around his neck.

"Mmm," he said, and bit her earlobe. "How far did you get today before your eyes started to cross?"

"Up to the 1840s. Great Mother, that woman wrote down everything." She arched her back as he massaged it, and her breasts rubbed against his chest. She was only wearing a shift, robe, and stockings, so his warmth transferred nicely to her skin. "That feels wonderful. Don't ever stop."

"I won't. But what if I want to…massage something else?" He pulled back to give her a wicked grin.

"That might also be acceptable, depending."

"On what?" he asked, but his hands were already sliding around to her hips and bunching her skirts to grasp the bare expanse of her ass. He kneaded the big muscles there, and she groaned. He answered her with a grunt, and then took her mouth in a demanding kiss. She thrust her tongue into his mouth, asking for what she wanted from him in the most carnal way possible without words.

Beneath her warm and already slick slit, his erection strained, and she rubbed herself against it. He clutched at the globes of her ass, his fingers curling around and stroking the delicate skin between her cheeks and down to where she already dripped for him.

A few buttons opened and his cock was free, and

moments later he was inside of her. They both sighed, and Etta broke the kiss to laugh.

"I love you." She kissed his nose, aiming for one of the many freckles dusted over it. He'd been out in the sun often this summer, studying geomancy and aquamancy with a Welsh mage. Each new freckle represented another day he'd been following his passion, as she now followed hers.

"And I you." He flexed his hips, pushing deeper inside her. They moved slowly, savoring the exquisite slide of his hard, hot flesh within her slick, tight depths. When release came, it was soft, and sweet.

Etta relaxed against Mal's chest. Little shudders struck them both from their still-sensitive skin, but she didn't lift her hips. She wanted him to stay inside her as long as he could. Her husband.

"I need to find out who is draining magic from England," she murmured into his shoulder.

"Muireall still might find a way to break the geas." Mal stroked a hand over her hair, the gesture only a little comforting.

"I won't risk passing it to our children." She didn't intend to get pregnant until her training ended, but she'd hoped they'd be able to start a family in a year or two at most. What if she never fulfilled Lilias's geas? Would her children be unwitting soldiers in their distant great-grandmother's war?

"We'll figure it out. Gwyn is already looking. He told me today that it isn't draining Wales or Cornwall as much, like it isn't pulling as hard from Scotland."

"That's so odd. Almost as though it is only English magic being targeted."

"Targeted, perhaps, but the rest of us are still effected."

Etta sighed, and pulled away. His cock had completely softened, and it slipped out with only the slightest of movements. She stood. "Eventually all of the magic will be gone, and we don't even know where it's going."

"We will. But it's going to be a massive project. A bigger spell than anything since Lilias and her group warded the entire British coastline from Napoleon. You're not ready yet, and we don't have enough support."

"Don't tell me I'm going to have to go court mages in London."

"I won't say it, but you already know it's true." Mal stood and wrapped his arms around her. "Mother and I are behind you, and so is the rest of the clan."

"Speaking of which, it's time we retrieved some things from Fay House. But I don't want Amelia and the queen to know what I'm doing, so none of us can go, and I don't want Sorcha coming here. Her Majesty has made it clear she doesn't want me to be a rallying point for English magic. She'd as soon the whole messy business disappeared from her shores."

"Ian has a friend. He's good at sneaking around. I'll arrange a meeting, and send him on to Sorcha."

"Good at sneaking? Who is this man?"

"His name is Ronan McCarrick. He's…well, he's a smuggler. And a thief. Probably a spy. Definitely a revolutionary. He's Irish."

"Great Mother. Her Majesty would have an apoplexy if she thought I was conspiring with the Irish."

"If we're going to succeed, we're going to need their mages. Muireall's already working on an exchange program with some of the magic schools in Dublin."

"Yes, I know. She was all aflutter about it when Evie started." Evie was a rapscallion of an Irish lass who'd recently begun attending classes, and Etta adored her.

"Ah, yes. Evie. She…used to run with Ronan's crew."

Mal looked a little sheepish about having withheld this

information so far, and Etta frowned at him a moment before giving up and laughing. "That explains a lot. I'll see if she can get in touch with him."

"Should we send word to Sorcha?"

"Better not. I'll write a coded and warded letter and send it with Ronan. I'm positive that our telegrams are monitored, and mail is as easy to open."

"We could try to contact her magically."

"That has its own dangers. And I want us better protected before we go public with what's happening to magic in England. We'll all be targets, then, from the people doing this and from anyone who would be happy that we don't succeed."

Mal squeezed her. "I won't let anything happen to you."

Etta laughed. "I won't let anything happen to you, either." She pressed her mouth to his, and they held each other tight. As long as they were together, anything was possible.

ON SKYE, IN THE ANCESTRAL HOME OF THE CLAN FAY, SORCHA Fay woke from a troubled sleep. A deep cold had settled within her, like a chunk of glacier lodged in her belly. Not so clear a warning as her visions usually provided, but something was about to happen. Some unknown tide had begun its turn.

Was it coming in, or going out? Would the change bring good fortune, or bad?

She got out of bed and checked the wards, a nearly unconscious habit formed over a lifetime as the guardian of this house.

The wards were out of alignment. Not by much, but more than should have been possible. Whatever was about to happen, this could not be a good sign.

THANK YOU!

Thank you so much for reading *Essential Magic*. I hope you enjoyed it.

- Want to know when my next book is coming out? Sign up for my newsletter at http://eepurl.com/bY89o1, like my Facebook page at https://www.facebook.com/caramckinnonauthor/, follow me on Twitter at https://twitter.com/cara_mckinnon, or sign up for release messages on BookBub at https://www.bookbub.com/profile/cara-mckinnon.
- Reviews help readers find books. Good or bad, I appreciate every one.
- *Essential Magic* is the first book in the Fay of Skye series. Book two is *A Theft of Magic*. Book three is *Memories of Magic. Secret Magic* and *Blood Magic* are forthcoming.

EXCERPT FROM A THEFT OF MAGIC

A woman sworn to truth. A man who deals in lies.
A passion lighting the way to love...or loss.

At the behest of the Duchess of Fay, Ronan McCarrick, thief, smuggler, and Irish revolutionary, travels to the Isle of Skye, the domain of Sorcha Fay. She is known as the Seeress of Skye, an elusive figure who rarely leaves the island. Ronan's arrival triggers one of her defensive spells, incinerating his clothing and everything he's carrying. Including the letter that would have told Sorcha why he has come to Skye.

Despite an instant attraction to the naked and furious Irishman, Sorcha believes that Ronan is an interloper who has been attacking her wards for months. Even when part of his story is confirmed, she still mistrusts him. But when she discovers that two powerful objects are missing from the Fay vaults—someplace he couldn't have been—she'll need his help to steal them back.

If he doesn't steal her heart first.

~

On the heels of the nightmare came the alarm from the wards.

Someone was trying to break into the house.

Sorcha Fay leapt from bed. She threw on her boots and her coat and scried the wards for the source of the alarm. The beach. She was halfway downstairs and headed for the back door before she even thought to be afraid.

Indignation and anger were the foremost of her emotions. She couldn't wait to confront whoever had been messing with her wards. This time, they were caught, and she'd prepared a few extra surprises in case they tried to escape.

Oh, she hoped they tried to escape. She might not be as quick on her feet with offensive spells as her cousins, but with plenty of time, Sorcha was perfectly capable of mounting an effective attack.

Or perhaps this was more accurately a defense—because she would defend Fay House to her dying breath. But with luck her dying breath would not come tonight.

She hurried down the cliff path to the beach, but stopped when her feet skidded against the small loose stones, making a terrible racket. She should be more wary. After all, whoever this was had tampered with her wards many times already, and she hadn't been able to track the source or trap the intruder before tonight. There was a not insignificant chance that even her skillful and malicious traps would be avoided or dealt with. She couldn't ignore the danger completely.

She used the salt spray, mist, and moonlight to weave a glamour. It would hide her until she could take stock of the situation, and she could take her time and place her steps more carefully the rest of the way.

The beach was a mix of sand and stone, and her boots made soft crunching sounds on the pebbles that she couldn't avoid without spending more time and magic, and she was impatient to confront her trespasser.

Assuming the intruder was still in the trap.

She came around a jut of cliffwall. A boat sat on the beach, beyond the water's edge. A few steps beyond the waves, at the base of the cliff, stood a man. Sorcha swallowed, hard.

He'd tried to use magic to escape, because her incineration spell had been activated in addition to the binding ward. It had worked exactly as she'd imagined, burning off his clothing and any items he'd been carrying. She'd meant the spell to leave intruders vulnerable, and bereft of any magical tokens they'd planned to use against her, but she hadn't been expecting her adversary to be so…male.

The moon was a hint shy of full, already sinking toward the west in the bright summer sky. Its pale glow and the never-quite-dark of a Scottish summer night illuminated the man's perfectly formed flesh, like a sculpture brought to life. He was tall and lean, with defined musculature but no bulk. He reminded her of a greyhound, with a powerful chest and shoulders but a trim waist and hips. Her gaze shied away from what was clearly visible between those hips and fled upward to his face.

Here, she stared—riveted. He was beautiful. She couldn't tell the shade of his eyes in the moonlight, but he had a long, straight nose and a thin, wide mouth. His cheekbones cast shadows onto the smooth planes of his face, and his jaw was angled and sharply defined. His hair was dark and much longer than was the fashion. He probably kept it pulled back, away from his face, but her spell would have destroyed any thong or tie. It whipped back from his face in the sea breeze, and when he swung his head as far as the ward would allow, a few strands tangled under his chin.

Something inside her belly burned. It was not fair that she would be attracted to this man. He'd invaded her sacred space, had come for a purpose that could not be good, and she was lusting after him as though he were an eligible lad from the village.

Sorcha clamped on her inconvenient desires and crept closer.

He was cursing in several languages. She recognized French and English, and that last was probably Irish because it sounded like Gàidhlig, but the pronunciation was off. His hand made an aborted gesture, probably another attempt at casting a spell-net, and when the ward reacted he suggested that it do something with itself that it did not have the proper appendages or orifices to accomplish.

In short, he looked delectable and dangerous, and Sorcha had no wish to confront him here in the open. So she drew down a few threads of the ward and rewove them, forming a new pattern.

"What in the hells?" the man shouted, as his feet dragged against the pebbled shore. This was going to be the tricky part. She'd had to sacrifice the extra protections to gain momentum, and she hoped he didn't realize that before she could maneuver him back into the little cave in the cliffs behind him.

Fortunately, he was too preoccupied fighting the motion to recognize that if he'd stopped and tried to rip the ward apart, he would have succeeded. She nudged him into the cave and quickly attached the ward to the stones around the entrance. Once she was satisfied with the new configuration, she tied it into the larger house ward so it would be sustained without her feeding it energy.

Only then did she let go, and drop her glamour.

～

Ronan McCarrick's night had started badly and gone straight to the hells. First he'd argued with Bart, the captain of his flagship, about the wisdom of going on this mission alone. He'd reminded his friend and smuggling-partner with more force than he'd intended who owned what and who called what shots. He'd then set off for the little cove nestled along the coastline of Skye.

He'd managed to muscle the longboat to shore over a choppy sea, while his ship disappeared into the night, headed south to finish its run. They would be back in a few days, depending on how the voyage went and how quickly they could dispose of their cargo. But he was on his own, and by the time he stumbled onto the beach his chest and shoulder muscles spasmed like fury.

Bart's prophecy coming true did not help his mood improve. The spell had sprung from nowhere. He'd strained against the threads of magic that had captured him, but though he could still move his upper body slightly, his legs had been immobilized.

Who the hells put such potent wards on a beach? With the wind and tide, the net would have to be renewed every day. Only an idiot or someone truly paranoid would go to such lengths to protect a stretch of sand and stone.

Annoyed, he'd flexed his fingers and prepared his typical counter-ward spell-net. But the moment he drew power into the first thread, the world burst into blinding light. He was bathed in heat, and then suddenly plunged into cold. It took a few moments for his vision to return, and when it did, the reason for the temperature spikes—and his now-pebbled flesh—became apparent. The ward had a countermeasure, which had incinerated his clothing.

Fecking hells.

Now he was naked, sore, and trapped on a frigid Scottish beach on a relatively deserted portion of Skye. He hoped whoever set the ward came to admire their handiwork. He intended to give them a scalding piece of his mind.

What sort of monster strips a man bare?

That was when it occurred to him that he'd had something rather important in his pocket. The damned letter to the Seeress, who would be unlikely to believe a random Irish stranger appearing on her beach in the middle of the night.

Bloody fecking hells.

He cursed until he could almost see the words hanging in the air, but it didn't improve his mood. How the feck was he supposed to escape this?

This was all Evie's fault. Damn her for running off and joining the Fay School and then luring him to help them with promises of the duchess's deep pockets. If she hadn't been like a sister to him, he would curse Evie to the dark god. As it was, he sent a fervent wish into the universe that every mug of ale she drank for a month went inexplicably flat.

Something pushed him away from the waves and toward the cliff. He flexed and wriggled as far as the ward would allow, but the pressure against his body was inexorable. His bare feet scraped through the sand and pebbles, and his curses were half in frustration and half in pain.

Darkness surrounded him. A cave, barely taller than he was, and not very deep or wide. He could see the back of the cave in the light of the moon, which had fallen far enough into the western sky to cast its illumination full in his face when he turned around.

The pressure ceased, and he stumbled forward against a force that was no longer pushing him. He fell. Inside the cave, the sand piled into deep mounds, with none of the pebbles from outside. It didn't exactly cushion his fall, but when he rubbed his knees, he was thankful that he had only minor abrasions and not jagged cuts.

The direct light of the moon illuminated the walls of the cave. Carvings and drawings surrounded him as though he'd wandered inside a standing stone.

He pushed to his feet and strode for the cave mouth. Another wall of force blocked his exit. He was tempted to try and break through with more magic, but he'd learned his lesson, and instead balled his hands into fists. He finally remembered to open his Sight, something he ought to have done the moment he landed on the beach. Then he'd not have gotten caught in the damned wards at all.

The ward was intricate and far too well-constructed for him to easily dismantle. The carvings on the walls glowed and hummed with magical energy, helping to feed the damned thing. He slammed one fist against his hip in frustration.

Beyond the barrier, shadow and mist swirled away to reveal a woman.

She was very short, with blond hair so pale it was indistinguishable from the moonlight. It was loose around her shoulders, and she wore a dark fitted coat, half-unbuttoned, over what looked like a nightgown. Was this his tormentor, then?

He couldn't distinguish her features. The moon at her back transformed her into a silhouette, limned by light. The sky wasn't truly dark, but it wasn't daylight either. Beneath the cliff there were too many shadows to see her clearly. She drew a symbol on the ward-wall, and though he hadn't missed the sound of wind and waves, it was a shock to have them return. How had she done that? He hadn't even seen the threads of the weave shift, and it still felt solid under his hand. If this was the Seeress of Skye, someone had lied about her proficiency with magic. She was bloody good.

"Who are you?" she demanded. "What have you been doing to my wards?"

$\sim$

Find out more about *A Theft of Magic* by visiting
caramckinnon.com/the-fay-of-skye-series.

ALSO BY CARA MCKINNON

THE FAY OF SKYE SERIES

Essential Magic (Etta and Mal)
A Theft of Magic (Sorcha and Ronan)
Memories of Magic (Olivia and Savit)

A Merge of Magic – A Serial Prequel
(Viola and Ian)
Amazon Kindle Unlimited Exclusive

COMING SOON
Secret Magic (Evie and Percy)
Blood Magic (Lucien and Rafe)

ANTHOLOGIES

Crazy Little Spring Called Love: Eight Magical Stories of Fantasy Romance
"Love at Dawn"

Love Across the Universe: Tales of Science Fiction Romance Set on Intergalactic Shores
"The Pirates and the Pacifist"

Love at the Edge of Seventeen: A YA Romance Anthology
"Three Jagged Pieces"

COMING SOON

Born to Love Wild: A Paranormal Romance Anthology
"A Change of Heart"

ACKNOWLEDGMENTS

A gigantic thank you to everyone who has helped bring this book to publication. My editor Anna LaVoie of Literally Yours Editing turned a muddle into a masterpiece. My dear friend and beta reader Mandi Hayes helped me brainstorm the events on Skye. Jamie O'Marr, Shelley Binder, and Christina Robbins gave great feedback on the cover art. My business partner, Jennifer Della'Zanna, has been a cheerleader and advocate during the entire writing process.

Getting my MFA was one of the best decisions I ever made, and the Seton Hill University Writing Popular Fiction community is inspirational and willing to answer all sorts of odd questions! Special shout-out to Shelley Adina who patiently replied to all of my nuts-and-bolts queries about independent publishing.

My eternal gratitude goes out to my SHU mentor, Maria V. Snyder, for teaching me how to be a better writer. Any lingering bad habits are my own fault!

This book would not exist without a lifetime of creative encouragement and support from my family. My parents told me to follow my dreams, and my husband and kids give me the time and space to write. I love you all!

And of course, a huge thank you to my readers. You make every hour spent worrying over word choice and learning obscure comma rules worthwhile.

ABOUT THE AUTHOR

Cara McKinnon has been writing magical stories since age five, when she penned a gripping tale about a unicorn couple —her first foray into fantasy romance. Cara is a graduate of the Seton Hill University Writing Popular Fiction MFA program, which she recommends to all genre writers. She lives in Western Maryland with her husband, two children, and an oversized lapdog named Jake.

Visit Cara online or send her a message. She loves to hear from readers!
caramckinnon.com
cara@caramckinnon.com

PRAISE FOR CARA MCKINNON

PRAISE FOR ESSENTIAL MAGIC

- "McKinnon writes clear and often beautiful prose, utilizing apt analogies to give liveliness to the text. An American girl with native blood who lands in London society makes a good frame for this romance novel." —Publisher's Weekly Booklife Prize (semi-finalist)
- "Vivid backdrop...thorough research...very hot. An entertaining start to a new series." –Avonna from The Romance Reviews
- "Engrossing and dramatic.... Tantalizing details... enough passion and excitement to carry along even the most non-romance reader." –J.L. Gribble, author of *Steel Victory*
- "The writing is just lovely.... Characters you care about!" –Maria V. Snyder, author of *Poison Study*
- "The romance is sweet and hot at the same time,

and the historical setting and details are beautifully done. Highly recommended." – Amazon review

- "[A] great romance." – Goodreads review
- "Masterfully written." – Amazon review
- "Cara McKinnon does a masterful job of transporting her readers to magical 19th century Scotland. Her detailed descriptions of historically accurate attire and etiquette helped to fully immerse me in a story that I was unwilling to put down until the very end. Engaging characters, powerful emotions; all with a unique and captivating method used to describe the casting of spells." -Christina Robbins, author of *Seeking Solace*

PRAISE FOR A THEFT OF MAGIC

- "McKinnon hits it out of the park once again with this delightful blend of alternate history, historical fiction, action, and sensuality...an exciting magical romp from start to finish." – J.L. Gribble, author of *Steel Victory*
- "Politics, schemes, and betrayal...twists that I definitely didn't see coming. The sex started early and got steamier as it went." – Dawn from Up Til Dawn Book Reviews for The Romance Reviews
- "The characters are beautifully crafted, the historical details make the world come alive and seem so vividly possible, I almost want to search for the missing magic myself." -Amazon review
- "What a superb fantasy historical! A great read that I shall keep and reread again and again. Her way of blending fantasy and magic with history was great.

I was captivated and enchanted and enthralled by her writing and her stories. I cannot wait to see what else she does. You will absolutely not be disappointed in buying this book or the series." – Goodreads review